I0552220

Clan Elves of the Bitterroot – Book IV

The Elf Guardian

Lyndi Alexander

Fantasy Novel Published by
Dragonfly Publishing, Inc.

This is a work of fiction. All characters and events portrayed in this book are fictitious. Any resemblance to real people or events is purely coincidental. All rights are reserved. No part of this book may be reproduced electronically or by any form or by any means, nor may it be rebound or performed without consent of the publisher and copyright holders. All eBook editions are sold under a standard single user license for the exclusive use of the initial retail customer and may not be copied, printed, changed, used for library lending, or distributed by any means for sale or for free to any other persons or business entities without the consent of the publisher and all copyright holders.

THE ELF GUARDIAN
Clan Elves of the Bitterroot – Book IV
Fantasy Novel released in 2013

Hardback Edition
EAN 978-1-936381-50-0
ISBN 1-936381-50-8

Paperback Edition
EAN 978-1-936381-51-7
ISBN 1-936381-51-6

eBook Edition
EAN 978-1-936381-52-4
ISBN 1-936381-52-4

Story Text Copyright ©2013 Barbara Mountjoy
Cover Art Copyright ©2013 Dragonfly Publishing, Inc.
Dragonfly Logo Copyright ©2001 Terri L. Branson

Published in the United States of America by
Dragonfly Publishing, Inc.
Website: www.dragonflypubs.com

Dedication

For my favorite geek, who made this book possible by going to the emergency room with a killer headache, and for my sister of the heart, Kellie, for making the trip out west with me so we could spend time in these magical forests.

Acknowledgements

With deepest thanks to my Pennwriters critique group—you are the best! It would be hard to keep producing stories without your support and sincere work and comments

Thank you to the folk at the Montana Vortex site in Columbia Falls, Montana for their help and assistance in researching this story.

I also appreciate the comments and letters of those who are reading the series—your support really inspires me to keep it going!

Thank you to Glenda Tudor, my editor and Terri Branson, who is more than just my publisher, but are both fans of these stories and their motley crew of characters. Thanks for sharing my vision and letting me share it with the world.

Most of all, I want to thank my husband Eric for all his work in collaborating, critiquing, mapping, charting, planning, reading and rereading these chapters, especially without stabbing me when I keep asking all those questions. It's better that way.

Special Terms

ELVISH DICTIONARY:
Denami: *Beloved*
Donoma: *What the elves call the Montana Vortex, the source of earth energy that they exchange with the clan, where their magic comes from.*
Elder: *Elves alive during the schism*
Idan: *Magical Element*
Idellan: *Balance of the six mages/powers*
Intalus: *Elven Mage*
Lelan: *The Clan, the People*
Nian: *Male elf*
Neris: *Female elf*
Santwarja: *Realm where mages train*
Younger: *Elves born after the schism*

ONLINE GAMER TERMS:
BSOD: *Blue Screen of Death*
DoTs: *Damage over Time*
PvP: *Player versus Player*
Toon: *Game Avatar*
MMORPG: *Massive Multiplayer Online Role Playing Game*

CHAPTER 1

THE phone line went dead before she could say goodbye.

Not that she would say goodbye, anything but.

"Hunter, wait—"

The once sweet name turned sharp and bitter on her tongue, as the whispered words sighed through her lips.

No, that was her teeth, biting down hard enough to make her bleed.

She set the phone onto its stand.

Gone.

Her knees gave way. She landed hard in her office chair and banged her elbow on the edge of the polished black and chrome desk. Pain radiated up her arm, but nothing seemed to cloak the agony raging inside her.

So close.

The news clippings spread across the surface of the desk seemed to mock her now. *Paranormal Investigator Visits Alcatraz. DeLuna Solves Local Murder with Psychic Clues. Ghosts Give Up Secrets to Ohio Paranormal Expert.* This was her life's work. Fifteen years of building a reputation as an investigator of the weird and unexplained. What would it count for if Hunter Nowles just walked away?

And why did he leave? Because that stupid exorcism had turned out to be a fake.

Okay, so the haunted old mansion in the Pennsylvania amusement park turned out to be a bust, too.

She chewed her lip. To be honest, she had failed to either prove or to debunk the last seven investigations. Lucky number seven.

"The great Chiara DeLuna bites the big one," she muttered, waiting for the rim shot that had to follow. It was a joke, right?

She was the joke.

The network seemed to think so. Davis sent a memo to her small sublet Midtown NYC office, warning her they would not fund her program if she could not produce results. Now Hunter had decided she was not worth his time, either.

Or maybe he was just afraid that her failures would taint his own growing stature in the paranormal investigation community.

Coward. Had their three years as lovers meant nothing at all?

Chiara stared out the window into the spring countryside as she picked at her hands. Only belatedly did she notice that her sixty dollar set of polished plastic fingernails lay scattered on the desk like dismembered victims of a ghost ridden murder scene.

I've got to get myself together. Now.

Her gaze was snagged by one of the news photos on the desk, herself smiling and shaking the beefy hand of some small town police chief. See? That woman was Chiara DeLuna, the *spooky* media star, tall, slender, chick platinum blonde hair, dark glasses, expensive wardrobe, and ominous black sedan that seemed to part crowds whenever she arrived on a scene.

Not the woman who looked back at her in the morning mirror. The gawky and bookish Bonny Lang from Euclid, Ohio. The same girl whose most thrilling accomplishment before hitting the 'big time' was as a teenager having barely survived a wreck with a drunk driver. Her leg had been broken and her pelvis crushed. Her mother died in the crash. Bonny sold her first paranormal article based on a post mortem conversation they had before her mother's spirit faded.

After that first spark of curiosity, she went on to study with mediums, took classes to develop her extra sensory perception, and read about all manner of bizarre occurrences to educate herself on the possibilities. In doing so, she found a niche as Chiara, turning her interest and predilection for the weird into a real moneymaker and finally achieving her own cable television show.

It might not have been one of the Big Four networks, but she had been famous enough to attract Hunter's interest, anyway.

Gone now.

She slumped in the chair. "What the hell am I going to do?"

"Did you read the memo I left you?"

Chiara noticed her intern standing in the doorway. Janie's blonde shag hair hung in her face and her worn jeans were too tight for polite company. In truth, she had not noticed any memo, not with being well on her way to 'Panic Land' and fearing she would be forced to return to life as Bonny Lang any day now.

"No," she responded, not wanting to share her ignominy.

"You should! Sounds like a hot lead." Janie flashed a grin and was off again.

Trying to marshal the energy to care, Chiara dialed her email on her smart phone with one finger. The memo caught her eye.

Montana Magic! A vortex found off the beaten path. It seems to have grown substantially in the last six months, affecting plant growth and climate. Half a dozen flares have been felt in nearby cities as well as the usual contained vortex areas, and no one exactly knows why. If this continues and the energy could be properly channeled, it could be the next Sedona.

Chiara was familiar with the spiraling, invisible energy of vortexes (*not* vortices, as her director kept trying to correct her). Their energy seemed to swirl right out of the surface of the earth, not magnetic, or electric, exactly, though it would register faintly as either in the most concentrated points.

Sensitives, of which she was one, resonated with this subtle energy. Even from a quarter mile away, it would actually interact with the energies contained inside the body to create a pleasant and mysterious experience.

She had spent three months and two episodes investigating the four vortexes in Sedona, those twisted juniper tree trunks climbing out of their centers sharing little jolts of psychic electricity that made her hair stand on end. If she could be instrumental in setting up the next big commercial spot where psychic energies healed and retuned people, she would be back on the road to her righteous place.

And Hunter would have to take me seriously again.

She sighed. Where was this place? It was in Columbia Falls, Montana somewhere in the great Northwest, almost to Glacier National Park. How fabulous. She hated mountains. She hated wilderness. She hated walking for miles, probably in hip deep snow, and most of all, she hated backwoods hotels without a decent menu or a clean hot tub.

Damn it.

What choice did she have?

She leaned back in her chair and bellowed. "Janie! Get me on a plane to Montana!"

CHAPTER 2

AS dusk approached, Max scrambled from one of the long fir branches to another, twelve feet off the ground, nearly invisible to anyone below.

Particularly any *human.*

Abandoned by his parents in the chaos following the murder of their previous queen, Max had hidden from the world since he was three years old. In elf years, of course. He had been all of four feet high then, his white hair, pale blue eyes, and pale skin making him unique, an oddity even in the Bitterroot elf clan known as the *Lelan.*

Max kept track of the part-elf, part-human male who scampered through the undergrowth, examining everything he could get his hands on. Unlike Max, that particular Younger would never have to worry about being left behind by his parents. Elliun, the young prince of their clan, was the son of elf queen Jelani Marsh and her consort Astan Hawk. Already, once, they had gone through the fire for Elliun.

They had fought for Max, too. The Circle, the elder females who advised the queen, argued against Max watching over and mentoring the young prince. They claimed Max was too strange, too immature to be trusted.

But Jelani's human friends, Lane and Crispy, advised her otherwise.

Although born only three years ago, Elliun was already the size of a seven or eight year old human boy. With a quartz rock in his hand, he looked up and immediately spied Max lurking in the shadows.

I didn't fool him at all.

"Will this sing for me?" Elliun waved the egg sized rock at Max.

Frustrated, Max jumped off the limb, letting his ability carry him lightly to the ground. From the time he was young, he had been able to fly, or more accurately, glide through the air. The Circle of elders said it was something in his bones, a gift from his odd heritage. Against the objections of the Circle, Psilea had trained and mentored Max.

If the Circle had their way, he would have been tossed on the mountainside to die.

Max examined the stone in the boy's hand. Though considered a young adult in elven terms, Elliun and Max were nearly the same height. For this reason, it helped them get along well. It was obvious that Elliun thought of Max as another child.

"What do you think? Will it sing for you?" he asked.

Elliun's lips curved into a smile. "If I want it to."

"Let's see. Make it sing."

Put on the spot, Elliun hesitated a moment before he turned his attention to the rock. Max hid his grin of triumph. Elliun had thought Max would do the work for him. *Not the proper role of a teacher, now, was it?*

Elliun stared at the rock, holding it flat on the palm of his hand. His face contorted with his effort, and, after many heartbeats, he finally frowned. "I can't."

"I disagree. You have the ability, Elliun, handed down from your mother. You have her resonance with all natural things. You can do this."

The boy sighed, setting aside his frustration to concentrate once again on the rock.

"Sense how the lines are drawn inside the crystal, in structured order, top to bottom, equidistant, one from the other." Max studied his pupil, reading the mental exertion he applied to the stone, even if he could not read Elliun's thoughts. If he worked at it hard enough, Elliun would sense the—

"Yes!"

They simultaneously felt the small jolt of energy pass through the crystal, at the moment when Elliun's mind connected with the invisible lattice within.

It was a beginner's lesson, merely to find the configuration and understand it. As Elliun's gifts developed, he would no doubt learn to alter that structure, as Jelani could, to improve the health of the land around them.

"Well done!" Max wrapped an arm around Elliun's shoulders and gave them a squeeze.

His face flushed, Elliun grinned and pocketed the stone. "I'm going to take it back to the tree house. I'll show my mother."

"Good idea."

The wind picked up with the coming of night, cool against Max's exposed cheeks. The fir branches overhead whispered the suggestion to return to the safety of the clan before darkness fell.

"Come on, Elliun. Let's head home. We've counted the elk herd on the western slope, climbed halfway up Goat Peak, and now you've made a rock sing. That's a good day's accomplishment for a *nian* of your age."

Elliun's shoulders suddenly stiffened, and at first, Max thought he would balk. But that did not seem to be his concern at all.

"My father's home," he gasped. "With Da!"

The sudden fervor in Elliun's voice kicked Max's heart into high gear. For several weeks, the clan had waited for Astan and his father, the mage Daven Talvi to return. While most summers seasons the Bitterroot clan would gather to recharge and exchange its energy at the side of *Donoma*, the energy vortex. But this year something was different. Something felt ominous.

As the clan prospered and expanded, especially this last year, the energy shared with the vortex had grown and fluctuated. Max overheard Daven tell Jelani that the vortex was losing containment, perhaps due to the earlier fractures in the social structure of the clan. Energy spikes had been released all over the Bitterroot, causing disruptions in human, as well as elven activity. They were very concerned.

He and Elliun started in the direction of the small enclave which housed the majority of the elf clan. It was an area the size of several 'blocks', as humans termed their paved subdivisions.

Not unlike the humans, elven housing rose above the ground many levels, magic constructing protected bowers in the tree branches that were home to many of the elves.

They had strayed farther than Max intended, so it took longer to get back. He found Jelani, her brow furrowed, as she watched anxiously from the stoop of the tree house Daven had enchanted for them. She wore a soft dress of green, her dark hair loose around her shoulders. To Max, she looked like one of the beautiful and regal queens on The Lane's computer game. Except she was not calm and distant. Instead her dark eyes flashed with annoyance.

"Where have you been?" Jelani scolded her son. "You kept your father waiting."

Elliun slowed to a walk well outside his mother's reach, his gaze flicking from her to the interior of the tree house. "He's not worried."

"No, that's my job," she growled, turning her burning gaze on Max. "And?"

Stung that she would rebuke him when nothing had gone wrong, Max stood as tall as he could. "He came to no harm, and we accomplished many lessons."

"Lessons?" Elliun's grandfather Daven stepped out from behind the tree, holding out his arms to the boy. "Tell me then, what you've learned that took a day from sunrise to sunset."

"I missed you, Da." The boy ran to Daven, and was swung up in strong arms. Max's pang of envy was quickly pushed aside. *I have a family, of sorts. I must accept what I have been given. The Lady of the Forest has not seen fit to grant me more.*

"Daven, don't spoil him," Jelani muttered, but it was too late. Elliun launched into his tale, regaling his grandfather with details of a day spent in the woods, full of natural wonders and ending with the singing stone.

Astan stepped into the doorway, his daughter Kayli in his arms. She was scarcely two seasons old, but already had the serious dark eyes of a Circle Elder.

"Sounds like time well spent," Astan said. "*Denami*, do not scold him. He was with Max. You know he will be well protected."

Daven grinned. "If this child continues to expand and grow as he has so far, he has the makings of a fine mage in him."

"What?" Jelani barked. "Let's not plan out his future already! He's only three."

"In our world, my queen, he is well on his way to becoming a young man." Daven's eyes held fond warmth. "As you know. All I'm saying is that he's doing well. We couldn't ask for anything more."

Astan gave Max an approving nod, echoed by Daven.

Thwarted, she sputtered a moment, and then pursed her lips in mock irritation. "Dinner is on the table. We should eat, now. Max, you are welcome to join us, if you'd like."

As much as Max would have liked to hear the news about the *Donoma*, he had other business he had put off all week while he attended to his duty to the queen, the clan, and young Elliun.

"No, thank you, my queen," Max replied.

Max performed a small bow that included the queen and the rest of her family before he took off running down the path that led, eventually, to Highway 93. He would continue along the road, well hidden among the trees. He could only guess what the tourists might think if they spotted his white hair in their headlights. Perhaps they thought him a lost antelope, or maybe even a ghost. He did not have time to dwell on such thoughts. He needed to be at The Lane's small apartment in the city of Missoula before the hour designated as nine p.m. by the humans.

Tonight was the quest.

CHAPTER 3

"YOU know, Crisp, if this keeps up, we're gonna have to buy another table. One of those eight seaters with the legs that fold out?"

Lane Donatelli surveyed the small apartment he shared with his long time roommate, Ron 'Crispy' Mendell. Over the past four years, since Jelani had left Missoula for the forest, they had not upgraded a stitch, except for a couple of new University of Montana coffee mugs someone had given them as a gift. Their five hundred square foot apartment had been invaded by four card tables, crowding their ancient furniture nearly to the walls.

Setting several six packs into the refrigerator, Kevin Briscoll just laughed. "Where the hell would you put that, Lane? There's no room in here now."

Crispy watched from the tiny hallway that led to the bedroom, leaning against the wall, arms crossed as though he could make himself invisible. As Lane and Kevin set up the tables, his lips pressed closer and closer together. Lane debated starting a countdown to when Crispy would explode.

Except that he would not. It was not his way.

Now, back in the day, Crispy was all manner of demonstrative emotion, letting his feelings run wild in flamboyant style, drinking, drugging, anything he could find to chase his reality away. No one liked living in an abusive home. Most liked living in foster care even less. That was where Lane and Crispy had met, in foster care. Both of them had survived hellish home lives, though they had coped with it differently.

Lane had found a devotion to sugary treats that assuaged his pain and built up layers of protection, literally and figuratively. Crispy had turned to less legal, more dangerous escapes. That was before he had gained the nickname, derived from the state of his brain once he finally crashed and burned.

"They'll be noisy," Crispy complained, before retreating into the bedroom.

Now *that* was his way. Withdraw. Retreat. Fade into nothingness.

Kevin joined Lane in the tiny living room. "Man, I hate to upset him. Why don't we have the raids downstairs in the shop?"

"Not like you have a lot of room either, with all those displays."

"Yeah, it's true."

Lane loved Kevin's small computer store, tucked into a storefront below their apartment. The front room was like a candy store for him, all the glitz and sparkle of new products and gadgets, and in the back room, a huge Beowulf cluster of computers that processed information for SETI and other projects. It was a geek's heaven. There was room in the back for one long table, where Lane taught beginning computer classes to Kevin's fellow National Guard veterans, many returning home from the wars in the Middle East, looking for new job skills. But that was it.

Once the news had spread that Lane and Kevin gamed together online, suddenly more wanted to play. And although the design of the MMORPG made it possible to play the same scenario individually in their own homes, somehow all of them playing together in one place made it a social occasion. By keeping it to twice a month, it made it tolerable for the usually antisocial Lane. But ten people in one small place at one time was not so acceptable to Crispy.

Compromise, always compromise.

"You could move," Kevin suggested.

The bedroom door slammed.

Lane grinned and shook his head. "Or not. We'll get through this. We survived the transition from WoW to TOR, right?"

"Mm-hmm." Kevin cracked open a beer and took a long sip. "I always knew you were drawn to the dark side."

"Evil overlord is in my genes."

"Too bad there's no elves in this one, though."

Lane shot Kevin a look. "I've got elves a-plenty in my life, thanks. Which reminds me, Max should be here soon."

"They all should be. I'll get the chips set out." He glanced toward the bedroom. "I thought he was better."

An uncomfortable snake of worry slithered through Lane's midsection. "He was. He *is*. It's just...maybe things have been too quiet. We've spent less time at the little house in the big woods, you know?"

"Never say things have been 'too quiet', brother. That's a recipe for trouble." Kevin knocked on the one wooden table in the room and went in search of bowls.

Damn. He's right. I should know better. Crispy always gets extra twitchy right before the metaphorical big log falls on the house.

Lane retreated to the Cave, his carefully constructed getaway inside their apartment. Four computers were ensconced in a space enclosed by walls built from an assortment of cardboard boxes, crates and storage bins. Once upon a time, his whole life had been centered within the artificial walls. In a way, it was very much like the 'safe' place Crispy had constructed, his agoraphobia keeping him inside the apartment until his therapist, and a generous helping of elven magic, had invited him back into the world.

Lane's egress into the greater world had taken a different form. Plopping down in his well padded manager's chair, he noted the blinking icon that indicated he had email waiting for him. Clicking on it, he revealed seven notes from fans new to his recently published digital book, *Queen Elf*.

He had taken the adventure he shared with Jelani, Astan and the others, and written a thinly disguised version of the story, careful to set it near Butte instead of Missoula to protect the clan's existence in the Montana woods. The manuscript had been rejected by a dozen agents as 'too outlandish', proving to Lane that truth was indeed stranger than fiction. Finally, he tapped one of his online gamer buddies to whip the manuscript into shape for electronic publishing, and he then published it himself.

Gamer friends had spread the word, and as they were a widely diverse group, they reached a lot of people. Lane had sold a good number of copies already, a fan base developing almost without his effort.

Now if I can only figure out how to leverage this into a fully paid appearance at the San Diego Comic-Con.

He started reading the emails aloud. *"Dear Lane, we loved your story. Can we come meet the elves?"*

"Dear Mr. Donatelli, I think it's sad that you perpetuate the fallacy of 'faerie folk' living in the forests of America, when everyone knows they only live in England."

"Dear Lane, can you write another story about your friends, the elves, but without so much violence, and with smaller words, so I can read it to my preschoolers?"

"Stop!" Kevin cried, laughing. "Please, stop. Where do these people come from?"

"Who knows?" Lane scowled and deleted the one from someone clearly just trying to act as a troll. *Enough negativity already out there in the world, pal. Sure don't need any more.*

"You getting rich off this book, dude?" Kevin perched on the bare edge of the desk, the only part with room to sit.

"Rich? Not hardly. But I sell a couple a week."

"That's something. Huh." Kevin rubbed his forehead. "You give any of it to the clan?"

"What would they do with money?" Lane asked. "Now that Jelly Bean's got them under control, all the prodigal elves have come home and been welcomed in, and the rest are producing the next generation. The more energy they have, the more they make for themselves. I'll bet Jelani hasn't been to town in four months."

"So what do you do with it?"

Lane laughed as a knock sounded at the door. "Pay Max's guild fees so he can play TOR." He shoved himself out of the chair and lumbered over to open it. As he suspected, the slight white haired elf waited on the other side.

"We were just talking about you," Lane said. "C'mon down!"

Max grinned. "Were you speaking of my brave exploits on your small screens?"

"Yes, pal. That's exactly what we were talking about." Lane let Max squeeze by his not inconsiderable bulk. "How's Elliun and the rest of the fam?"

"He is well. The others prepare for the *Donoma*." Max skidded over to the table, taking several nacho flavored chips from the basket Kevin had just set down. He held one up and licked the flavoring off it. Then tossed the naked chip into the nearby wastebasket, before doing the same with the next one.

Lane eyed him, mystified. "You're weird, man." He sighed. "The *Donoma*, huh? That's coming up. Astan reminded me last time we spoke. As a mage of the clan, I suppose I'll have to come up and lend my bit of magic to the proceedings."

Kevin snorted. "What exactly will the legendary technomage of the Bitterroot clan contribute to the ceremony? The point of the ritual is to connect to natural energies, right? Not something that runs through your servos and wires."

"Damned if I know." Lane shrugged. "Daven says it's a matter of balance. He wants all six mages present this time, along with the queen, in order to pull off the event. I guess it's more than the usual annual backup and reboot. This vortex thing receives the gift of energy from the clan, some kind of tribute, and then the energy flows back onto the clan, all cleansed and recharged."

Kevin just stared at him. "Right."

"Hey, this is Daven's gig, not mine. I'd be more worried about his ex showing up to wreck the day than anything I could do to the process."

"Still sounds sketchy to me."

Lane rolled his eyes. "Max, tell him. This is for real, right?"

Max dragged himself away from a handful of cheese puffs with a regretful sigh. "Of course it is for real. Now that the clan is one again, the ebb and flow of energy should be in harmony with the earth. By celebrating that connection, we all receive the gift of life."

"See? The gift of life. Keeps the natives happy and me a lot closer to home more of the time." Multiple knocks sounded on the door and he went to let his guests in. "Hey, how ya doing? Come on, it's nearly time."

Half a dozen of their raiding buddies filed in, each bearing a food or drink item in addition to their laptop cases. Max borrowed one of Lane's extra laptops and took a seat at the end of the table as the others set up. Lane kept an eye on the screen as Max manipulated the keys and programs with his own unique abilities, intuition showing him how to make the machine work without formal training. Max opened one browser window to the game, but while he waited for the others, he opened a second to YouTube, where he searched out old Three Stooges clips, laughing uproariously at the trio's antics.

Lane chuckled as he made his way into the Cave, a cup of hot Earl Grey in hand and a box of Creamy Cupcakes in the other. "In the famous words of my hero, Jayne Cobb, let's be bad guys!"

The others cheered as they settled into their seats, their own preferred libations in hand. Most of them did not know that three years before Lane and Max had pulled off a miracle, ending the clan's quarter century civil war when Lane had enchanted one of his video game characters and had drawn it into the real world to fight the evil elf overlord.

But that was all right.

Sometimes those strange truths got in the way of people considering one a down to earth kind of guy. Lane had spent so many years on the outside of 'normal' life looking in, that in this particular instance, he gave himself a pass. He saved his war stories for his times among the elves. It was enough. No need to relive those days, as long as the Bitterroot clan remained at peace up there in their big woods.

CHAPTER 4

THE next morning, Lane found something a little out of the routine, an email from a woman named Chiara DeLuna, who introduced herself as a 'paranormal investigations professional'.

Lane shook his head as he read the email.

First off, if your title includes the word 'professional' I'm going to think you're a little insecure. And if you're that insecure, you probably don't know what the hell you're doing.

And if you're coming to ask me for help, then I think maybe we're both on the trail to Pretty Well Lost.

He read it again, strictly for entertainment value. "Dear Mr. Donatelli: Perhaps you know my name, Chiara DeLuna, Professional Investor of all things paranormal and weird? My television show on the YES cable network has won several awards, and I have busted myths and legends around the country and also on an international scale. In researching my latest project, I find that not a lot is available on mystical happenings in your local forests, other than the usual Native American spirit legends. I know your book is fiction, but something about the way you tell this story shows me you know more than you're sharing about what goes on in those deep, dark woods. The Montana Vortex is located just north of the area you wrote about. Are you familiar with this? I'm thinking of featuring this site in one of my upcoming programs. If you'd be willing to be interviewed, I'd love to spend some time picking your brain. You could be one of my on screen sources, maybe even get in a plug for your book. What do you say? I'll be in Missoula in a few weeks, and I'd love to get together and buy you a drink. Or coffee, maybe, at that little Butterfly coffee shop you wrote about? I've included my cell phone number and email address. I'll be waiting to hear from you."

She signed her name with a little circle above it. Or was that a halo?

Lane chuckled. "Oh, lady, if you only knew what I could tell you about those woods."

"What woods?" Crispy asked from the kitchen.

Lane could not see him, but he heard the spoon dinging against the sides of the metal pitcher Crispy had bought at a thrift store years ago. He was probably making another batch of pomegranate green tea, without sugar, which tasted like fresh cut grass shavings. It would not be so bad, but Crispy insisted Lane drink it too, because it was 'good' for him.

Right up there with the Jim Jones cool-aid in my estimation.

Besides that, Lane was a man who lived for Creamy Cupcakes. Did he really look like he worried about what was good for him?

Just thinking about the brew made Lane shudder, as he leaned back in his chair. "You know. *The* woods. Jelani's woods. Some fakey ghost hunter is asking for my help in divining the mysteries of the woods. Guess she heard about the Vortex and—"

Crispy's face popped around the corner of the wall. "She's not coming, is she?"

Lane frowned. "So what if she does, Crisp? She'll hit that place up in Columbia Falls, get her picture taken with a friend, showing her growing and shrinking, and maybe get a few chills up her spine. Walk the labyrinth. No biggie."

"The Vortex? This summer? Hello?" Crispy disappeared. He returned in a moment with two frosty glasses and handed one to Lane. "What about the ritual? She could steal the elves' souls!"

"She can't steal the—well I don't think she can steal the...." Indecision softened his jaw. "I mean, do they even have souls?"

Crispy just eyed him. "Not the point."

No, he supposed it was not. This wasn't the time for arguing about angels waltzing on a pin or other religious claptrap. His Jelly Bean had a way of attracting a lightning strike of bad luck like any metal pole on top of a barn, and this might just be the latest example. The last thing the Bitterroot clan needed was exposure on some hokey cable psychic extravaganza.

He set the glass down as far away as he could while still pretending he would get to it shortly. "Guess it's time for a road trip."

"Are you sure she's coming?"

"She said she was. Hmm." Another idea occurred to him, something that involved his own charm and particularly devious tactics. "Maybe I can head her off. After all, I took on Bartolomey with a bunch of magic charged pixels. How much worse could this prima donna be?"

Crispy chewed his lip, his foot tapping in a staccato pace. "You should tell Jelani and Astan."

"Agreed. Let me see what this harpy really wants first. Maybe I can send her on a wild snipe hunt." He winked, but Crispy did not relax an inch.

Kevin was right. Crispy wasn't getting better. He wasn't getting better at all.

"I'll let you know what she says, okay, Crisp?"

Crispy took a long drink of his tea. "Then you should warn them. We can't let her take Elliun."

Exasperated, Lane held out the letter. "No one said anything about Elliun. She just wants to know about the ooga-booga stuff. Have you ever seen this woman?" When Crispy did not take the letter, he dropped it onto the desk and turned to the second of his four slaved computers, and ordered it to search for the lame woman's show. "Look at her."

Crispy edged closer, avoiding the lens of the web cam, and peered around the corner at the monitor's wide screen, which displayed a tall woman who could have walked a Hollywood red carpet, tall, platinum blonde, wearing heels that had to be four inches tall and a skirt that did not seem much longer, if the expanse of leg in between was any indication.

Lane found his gaze distracted by those legs, especially because the photo was shot at an angle as if the cameraman was kneeling down low, not an up the skirt angle but something a little more queen of the world. He did not know much about fashion, but the jacket and skirt Chiara wore had that bland, useless look in an off green color that had to mean it cost twice as much as any normal person would pay for it.

Lane rolled his eyes. What did he know? He did his shopping at the local thrift store.

"She'll fall down," Crispy commented.

"In those shoes? You betcha. Take her on one of those hikes like Jelly dragged us on. We'll see how much magic she finds, right?"

They both laughed.

"All right, Crisp, don't worry, all right? I'll handle this. Just…." He edged the glass of tea away just a little. "If I'm doing serious work, I need to have something real to drink. Nourishment, you know. Tall glass of milk, and a double pack of cupcakes. I promise it's just the right amount of rocket fuel to get my engines revving."

He gave Crispy a winning smile. "P-P-P-lease?"

Crispy drew in and let out a long, exasperated breath. "Fine. I'll get you milk, but I'm leaving that tea there. It'll relieve the problem you're having with constipation."

What? Lane blinked from the blindside comment. "What? What are you talking about?"

Crispy stepped into the kitchen to get the snacks. "Don't be shy with me, bro. How long have we lived together? Almost ten years? When you're not worried and torn up about something, you're a seven a.m. every morning guy. The last week and a half, after Daven asked you to come up on the mountain to help plan this ritual? You're not even every day. Keep it up and you'll explode."

He came back with the items and cocked his head. "And I'm not cleaning it up when you explode. So drink the tea." Crispy stepped back, fidgeted a little, and then headed for the door. "I'm going to pull weeds."

Weeds? Crisp had three tomato plants and some beans.

Lane shook his head. At least his roomie was outdoors

instead of trapped in his room. *Quit while you're ahead, Lane.* He eyed the computer again, thinking this woman had to be out of her mind. She wanted to get together? She wanted to learn some crazy secrets about the woods? He was nothing if not all about crazy.

He ripped open the cupcakes and started to type a reply.

CHAPTER 5

"WHAT if Veraena doesn't return?"

Jelani gritted her teeth, digging her fingernails into the apple on the table. Djana had been at this series of questions for the last hour, drilling her about the upcoming ritual as if it was her first day on the job as queen of the Bitterroot elf clan, not four years into it. If her mate Astan was here, he might have diverted his grandmother, but he had gotten one up on Jelani, by deserting her the first thing that morning with a peck on the cheek and a wink.

"Don't give her too hard a time, *denami*," he teased, wagging a finger in her direction. Then he opened the door of their magic tree house and escorted Max and Elliun out for a day in the forests.

Djana cocked her head, her sharp brown gaze skewering Jelani. "Well?"

Jelani studied the old elf woman, seeing she looked almost young again. Since the schism in the clan had healed, the old evil mage Bartolomey destroyed once and for all, and the *Lelan* coming together under her rule, the energies that fed the clan flowed strong from the earth, and the balanced group of proper mages channeled those energies back in a never ending cycle. The abundance of positive energies rejuvenated the clan and even helped to heal the very land about them. Crispy had quoted some of the park rangers talking about how this was a bonus year for not only plant and tree growth but also wildlife as far north as the Kootenai National Forest and as far west as Coeur D'Alene.

And all because I finally came home where I belonged. Just in time to become Djana's nagging post.

She sighed. "She'll come, Dee. Everyone knows how troubled the *Donoma* has been in the last several months. Even if she doesn't want to live with us, her sons and her grandchildren are here." She shot Djana a look. "Elf women do care about their grandchildren, right?"

Djana dropped the ball of yarn she fiddled with onto the table. "But—"

The door opened, cutting off her question. Though Jelani was not expecting anyone, she would have been happy even to see Lane's drooling demon warrior manifestation if it would have shut up Djana.

It was Daven, *the next best thing.*

He must have sized up the tension in the room, because a smile moved slowly onto his lips, inching there like a caterpillar along a branch. He grinned at Jelani. "Making apple salad?"

She dug her nails out of the innocent fruit and cut it with a knife instead. "Exactly."

Djana wasted no time in an effort to monopolize her son's attention. "I was just discussing with Jelani the importance of the ritual and the need to make sure the mages attend. All of them."

"Why wouldn't they, Mother? All of us have experienced the instability of the energy field, and each one of us depends on the energy it provides and receives. Even the Mages. I'm sure we can count on all of them to do their duty."

The broad shouldered elf snagged a few chunks of apple off the table and plopped himself into the nearest chair. His hair had grown long and thick, not a shred of gray in it, even though he was nearly a hundred by human standards. Jelani did find him good looking, but her heart completely belonged to his son, Astan. All those petty jealousies that had gotten in their way years before had fallen by the wayside now.

"Our duty to the clan keeps us united," Jelani added, cracking some nuts into her bowl.

Daven grinned. "Now who'd have thought you'd be the one spouting Circle doctrine, dear?"

Jelani shot him a look. "I lead the Circle, don't I?"

He inclined his head. "You are our queen."

"Exactly." She caught Djana's curdled expression from the

corner of her eye and smiled. Nearly five years after Jelani had been charmed into her first contact with her elven family by Djana's cheesy glass slipper trick, the old *neris* still resented losing her position as top female. She had become much less vocal about it, of course, and in company she kept a complacent smile on her face. But it always seemed clear that the battle was not over.

I'll outlast her, if it's the last thing I do.

Daven seemed to ignore the low grade tension between the two. "Iris is excited about coming to the ritual this year. She's cleared her schedule for the whole weekend so she can stay in the woods."

"What you see in a human woman," Djana muttered. Both Jelani and Daven glared at her, and she quickly pressed her lips closed before more complaints escaped.

Jelani felt she had to stick up for her best friend, whether Iris Pallaton would have been insulted or not. "What he sees in this particular human woman is a strong heart, one that loves him without any question. Iris gave countless hours of her time during the year it took to heal the hurts of our clan, negotiating and counseling with the various factions until everyone came to consensus."

More hours than I had patience for, Jelani recalled. Fortunately, she had other duties to excise from the Circle's grasping hands, duties that properly belonged to the queen, and so she could be excused from some of the more tedious sessions.

"She honestly cares for the well being of our clan, even if she'll never be a full member."

Jelani glanced at Daven, knowing his heart was in this as well. After he mated the first time, a mistaken alliance with Astan's mother Veraena, he had refrained from rash judgments about commitment. He had suffered so many years for his duty to the clan. He said he wanted any future permanent bonds to be well thought out and held for the right time.

But he has been seeing Iris for three years now. Surely it will be time soon for him to make a serious commitment.

Daven cleared his throat. "I think it's clear in the last several seasons that humans can be valuable to the clan. Perhaps it made sense a century ago for elves to blend seamlessly into the forests and keep themselves separate, but humans have spread into nearly every area that the elves once held. We can't ignore them any longer."

Djana sat a little straighter, her voice now a honeyed tone. "Of course not, dear. Look what the addition of human blood has done to our royal line."

She eyed Jelani, who only grinned.

"Looks like it's given your line a backbone and a will to get things done." Jelani finished mixing her salad and slipped it into the cupboard naturally cooled by an underground stream below. In the Bitterroot, it often snowed right through Memorial Day. There were not too many days when heat would spoil food inside her magical space.

Daven agreed with a nod and a grunt. "Speaking of humans, Lane and Crispy are coming along, right?"

"All the mages need to participate in order to achieve balance, even the technomage wonder boy." She chuckled. "I'm sure he'll bring some dazzling display of pyrotechnics or some offbeat recording of the *1812 Overture* or something to contribute."

"It will be unique. I'm sure, just like he is." Daven got up from the chair, walking over to peek in the wooden cradle near the fireplace where Kayli slept.

"Don't you wake her up. It took me an hour to get her to sleep."

A quill in hand, Djana tapped an exasperated foot. "Can I verify final preparations. Then I'll leave you two alone?"

Her meal preparation complete, Jelani felt a moment of guilt at not being more tolerant of Djana. "I'm sorry, Dee. Let's look at this again." She joined the older neris at the table and studied the list they had prepared so far. "The members of the clan will travel to the *Donoma* site, each bringing his or her gift to the earth. The six mages will each provide their own donation and illumination to complete the ritual."

"Midsummer also brings out the pagan humans as well, so we will have to take care to avoid them," Djana warned.

"They often don't see us anyway," Daven interjected. "They are too busy with their eyes on what's right in front of them."

Djana nodded and continued. "As important as this particular ritual is to the year round well being of the clan, however, it would seem an extraordinary amount of caution would be best."

"I'm sure everyone will be careful, Dee." Jelani tapped the list. "We've taken into account the height of the western mountain in calculating the moment of dusk?"

"Within several minutes. It will be approximate, but close enough. When we reach that moment—"

"I know, I know. Daven will speak. Then I, as the queen, will call the clan to convene as one, bringing them home for the ceremony. Then each of the mages will perform their part of the ceremony, pulling the *Donoma* back into place."

"And we initiate the new queen," Djana said quickly.

Jelani scowled. This was still something she had not resolved to do. She glanced over at her sleeping daughter. "She's not even two. I don't think she'll be taking over any time soon."

"Yes, but we know what happened when your father took you from the forest without consecrating you in the proper ways, solidifying your connection with the clan and the earth. You lost your way, and we nearly lost you."

"Those circumstances were totally different! You had a homicidal elf on the loose and—"

Daven cleared his throat. "Can we save this part of the discussion until Astan is here? As Kayli's father, he should have something to say about it."

The two women glared at each other, and Jelani let it drop. She did not want the Circle polluting her baby's mind with any kind of pap, especially all that garbage they tried to shove down her throat when she had first come to the clan.

On the other hand, if she grows up in the bosom of the clan, she'll already know so much more than I did. She won't need all that indoctrination well past her college years.

Daven waited until the silence became deep enough to be called a truce, and went on. "The best part of the ritual will come. When we have shared in the gifts of the mages, when the energy source of the clan is once again realigned. Then we will recharge ourselves as well."

With warm fondness reminding her, Jelani thought back to the previous years, the rush of power that came up through the ground into their feet, their legs, moving through their bodies like a blast of liquid lightning. The swirling force collected inside the circle of joined hands for only a moment, and then released itself vertically and horizontally into the other living beings around them. This ritual had resurrected several nearby copses of fir trees, previously dying, that had restocked the rivers with fish and the air with birds no one had noticed in the area for fifty years. The power of the elf clan resonated within and without, bringing their world to a higher level. That rush was the best high ever.

If only it could be packaged and sold.

Stop that.

She had talked about it with Lane once. He had been all fired up about the magical flow and the experience. *"We'd be zillionaires, Jelly Bean,"* Lane had promised. *"Just set up junkets to come here to get a jolt."* But Jelani had reminded him how many long years it had taken for the clan to recover from the chaos created by death of her mother, the previous queen. There was no way she would jeopardize the clan now. No way. Lane was disappointed, but muttered something about people at least being able to experience the benefits from the vortex at the formal gateway in Columbia Falls. His reluctant agreement was still his word. That was good enough for her.

Djana was still talking, wrapping up the plan for the ceremonial evening. Everything seemed to be as it had been the several years before. Another two weeks, and their entire clan would be recharged and ready to face another year of prosperity, good health and strong magic.

Everyone was onboard. How could anything go wrong?

CHAPTER 6

ON Sunday night, the third week of June, Chiara waited impatiently for her suitcases to come off the plane and onto the baggage carousel.

Even the natural beauty of the Missoula airport terminal, its high ceilings supported by gently curved wood beams, could not distract from her annoyance. Most travelers adapted to the stringent post 9/11 air travel rules by condensing what they brought on their journey and stuffing it into mostly carry on bags.

But professional paranormal investigator Chiara DeLuna did not travel that way. She needed her flamboyant clothes, her set of wigs, and her 'tools' of the trade, along with enough makeup to cover the damage of age. And her jewelry. Do not forget the jewelry. She had to look expensive, because that was who Chiara DeLuna was.

Old Bonny Lang might be a dowdy old maid, but Chiara was *fabulous*.

That's how it has to be if you want to hold on to the network show, the costly gigs, and the man you love, right?

She sighed, thinking of Hunter. How he would have loved this. Tromping through the woods and scaling mountains. Or like that one movie which was set in Montana, where they fished in hip boots and winged their poles back and forth as if chasing away flies. *Must be why they call it fly fishing.*

This little adventure would prove to him she was worth his love, though. She was sure of it.

She had spent the last two weeks poring over maps, even reading articles written by others who claimed to debunk the Vortex as a magical source of energy. All of those were at least seven years old. No one had been here recently. Probably they discarded the idea in light of all those negative reviews, without looking at the whole picture. Instead, Chiara used her considerable charm to woo park rangers and local environmentalists over the phone, name dropping all over the network, gathering tidbits about the strength readings near the vortex, and the general fifty percent increase in the health and welfare of everything around the site.

And I could get out there and see it for myself, if I could just get my stupid luggage!

Once she had her missing baggage, she would find a rental counter, get a car, and head out to the hotel. *With any luck, they'll have decent coffee in the room at least.*

"Miss DeLuna?"

A male voice came from behind her, holding just the right note of wondrous respect. Something clicked in Chiara, reminding her she was a star. She turned around, her shoulders straight, a distant smile on her lips. "Yes?"

The first thing she noticed was his height. He was tall. Even though she was wearing three inch heels, he stood eye to eye with her. Wide set blue eyes highlighted a perfectly proportioned, a well tanned face, and jet black hair cut in military style. He wore a green polo shirt and khakis over a pair of hiking boots. This guy was a hunk! His sense of calm, self assured presence rolled over her like an ocean wave, rattling her carefully cultivated distance.

Something in his eyes changed as he watched her. Was that a hint of amusement?

He knew.

Somehow he had read her, understood the effect he had on her.

"Have we met?" She cleared her throat, waiting for some explanation of why he had approached her.

He held out a hand, acting perfectly normal, as if pretending he had not shaken her world. "You're even prettier in person. I'm Curran Tanner. We spoke on the phone about the Montana Vortex site?"

She seized on the name, flipping through her mental file folder for a reference. Right, he was one of the local environmentalists. He had not looked so tall in the picture on his webpage. She took his hand and shook it warmly.

"Curran, so nice to meet you. I had no idea you'd come to the airport to meet me."

Now that she thought about it, she was pretty sure she had not told him she would be at the airport at all. How had he tracked her down? *Stalker* whispered through her head.

He laughed. "No, that was my idea. I'd called your office and your girl Janie told me when you'd be arriving. I didn't know if you'd rented a car yet. I thought maybe we could trade favors. I'd drive you up to your hotel if I could pick your brain about a few things."

"A car. Right. I was going to rent a car."

But I hadn't got to that yet because I can't seem to find my luggage. Wait. Just as she finished her thought, her two large bags came sliding down the silver ramp into the carousel. A sigh of relief escaped her.

"Are those yours? Let me help," Curran said. Before she could even lift a hand, he had crossed the distance to the carousel with his long legs and grabbed their handles without even a grunt of effort, setting them carefully on the floor. "Any more?"

She gestured to the two small cases she had with her, which held her most precious items, her laptop, a small video camera, and other electronics. "This is it."

Curran grinned. "So, what do you say? Do we have a deal?"

* * *

THE trip north on Highway 93 seemed to go on forever, and in the end, Chiara was deeply grateful she agreed to let Curran drive her up. What was apparently the only road to Glacier and the other northwestern cities was hopelessly clogged with traffic, families of summer tourists packed into their bright SUVs driving alongside huge trucks loaded with thick pine logs. She would have plucked her head bald from nerves if she had to navigate it herself.

"You could have flown into the airport at Glacier," Curran

scolded her gently, after she complained for the fourth or fifth time. "It may be small, but it's perfectly adequate for this sort of thing. Then it would have just been twenty minutes out to the lodge."

"My airline didn't fly there." She did not add that the airlines that *did* fly there had banned her from ever taking them again after various incidents over the years. *Not my fault if they don't understand the meaning of 'star treatment'. I have my own television show, you know. I may not have won an Emmy yet, but surely it's coming.*

"It's hard these days, it's true. All the airport security hang ups and the lines. I'm surprised anyone flies at all."

"You're not kidding." Chiara gaped out the window. Spectacular mountain vistas lay on every side. They came to Flathead Lake, driving up the west side with its vacation homes and small restaurants and art shops to the left, the broad blue expanse to the right, a picture postcard setting with dark green pine in the background, flanked by the nearly black Mission Mountains. Even to her jaded eyes, it was gasp-worthy. She tried not to act like a dumb hick from flat old Ohio.

"Fantastic, isn't it?" Curran spared a glance for the view before he set his gaze back on the road. "When you first called, I thought maybe you were looking for Nessie."

"Nessie? Like a Loch Ness monster?"

"So they say." He chuckled. "I've never seen her. But plenty of others say they have."

She might have noted something about that in her research, but apparently had not focused on it. Instead she centered her attention on this vortex issue. But all the same, what if? Too bad her video equipment was packed in the trunk. Just in case, she dug in her purse for her smart phone and made sure it was charged. *Any little bonus helps.*

"So you're going up to the Grand Pheasant Lodge? Ever been there before?"

"I've never been to Montana before. I mean, except for the Bigfoot investigations, there really hasn't been much of interest out here."

His jaw tightened for just a moment, but he did not look away from the road in front of them, maneuvering around a slow moving, dilapidated red pickup truck. Chiara glanced over at the pudgy, bespectacled driver, occupied in an argument with his floppy haired passenger, the strains of rock music blasting out his open window. They were more long haired, hippie, tree hugger types. She had noticed a lot of them at the airport as well. There were probably as many granola eaters there as out in Portland, where she had once investigated a haunted hotel, or Denver, or even Sedona. Sweet heaven, give her New York any day. There was plenty to do, day and night, and people who knew who she was. She could get a table at most of the best restaurants in town with a phone call. Now that was useful.

A moment of silence fell between them and then Curran carried on with a note of determination in his voice. "The Lodge is really nice. I've stayed there for skiing weekends, but never in the summer."

"The amenities seemed to be pretty good."

"Amenities, right." He stared straight ahead.

She glanced at him. His warmth had surely worn off. *Probably something I said.* She tried to run through their conversation, but could not identify anything particularly hostile. *I've just got too much riding on this. I've got to pay better attention. Get back on track with this guy.*

"What's your favorite area up here in the mountains, Curran?"

"Lake McDonald is beautiful. The glaciers carved out this huge valley with snow topped mountains all around it. The place is stunning any season, though it's most accessible in the summer. The Going-To-the-Sun Road is scheduled to open next week."

"Going-to-the-Sun?"

"It's named for the Going-to-the-Sun Mountain in the north end of the park, which comes out of a Blackfoot tribal story passed down through the generations. The Road goes from the western entrance of Glacier across the Continental Divide to the east end."

Smelling the possibility of a story here, with a mysterious closed road in a national park, she got ready to make notes. "What's happened that they couldn't open it?"

Curran just grinned at her. "It never opens until midsummer. Logan Pass usually has about eighty feet of snow left in the spring. It takes weeks and weeks for the Park Service to clear it all out, even with their specialized equipment."

Eighty feet of snow.

The thought totally baffled her imagination. As a child, she had lived right inside the Snow Belt on the east side of Lake Erie, so she knew about snowfalls, but the most she could ever remember seeing was maybe three feet at once. Sometimes drifts around buildings of five or six feet. Eighty feet? As tall as a seven story building? The concept boggled her mind.

"Will we see that from the road here?"

"No, it's up in the Park. But not too far from the Lodge. I can drive you in to places where it will be much closer. Maybe half a day's hike."

Half a day? Walking? She swallowed hard and bit her lip to keep the dismay from shoving its way through her teeth. This was the Wild West, after all, not Manhattan. People still walked, on purpose.

"You wouldn't believe the wildlife you'll find, though. I nearly ran afoul of a herd of elk once. Luckily, I managed to get to some trees for cover and I was downwind. A bunch of new calves were in the herd and the mothers might have trampled me if they'd thought I was a threat."

"Elk?" She pictured elk as somewhat tall, giraffe like deer, with long legs, small brains like cows, dull witted, and only interested in food. She never thought they could stomp someone to death. "I didn't know they were violent."

Curran laughed. His good humor restored. "They're not violent animals. The mothers just go to any length to protect their children against threats. Like any of us." He adjusted the air conditioning dial. "I'd do the same for my son, Will."

Another pause, as if he were inviting her to share a bit of

personal detail. That was too bad. The mention of a child only reminded her that she would never have children. The accident long ago had seen to that. But it was a reminder she did not want. "Well, you're a good dad, then."

"Thanks. I like to think so. I thought, if you were interested in having a guide, I'd volunteer. Maybe Will can come along."

Maybe he can cart me back when I fall over dead at the end of the day from all that sweaty exertion.

"Sure, that would be nice," she said.

She talked him up the rest of the way to the Lodge, trying to pull details about this mystical vortex from his experience, but he kept turning the conversation to engage her in general discussions about the beauty of the entire Bitterroot area. He suggest places he could take her that she just 'had' to see, like the Trail of the Cedars, apparently inside Glacier National Park, or the National Bison Range.

"Yaak Falls. That whole Yaak River area is definitely something you should see before you go home. How long did you say you'd be here again?"

"As long as it takes," she said, forcing a smile. "Like I said, my main focus is the vortex."

"But there's so much more." He sighed. "I'm sorry. I just love to share this area with people who've never seen it before. It helps me recapture my own wonder upon seeing it for the first time. But don't mind my enthusiasm. We'll see how your time plays out."

"Thanks." She relaxed into the seat a little, glad that Curran's regular job as a lobbyist paid well enough to get him a very comfortable Enclave, instead of some rickety beater, like half the cars on the road. "My camera crew should be here Friday night. I just wanted to be here a few days early, scope out the site, you know."

"Sure, that's understandable." He turned off the highway at the sign indicating the way to the Grand Pheasant Lodge. The driveway led to an immense facility at the bottom of a mountain, whose wood walls and smoothly curved roof sections almost made it feel like it was an extension of the mountain itself. The resort rose above the portico four floors, looking more like something one would find in Switzerland or Germany rather than crass America. Chiara had to admit she was impressed.

"Pretty nice, I know," Curran said, popping the trunk for her luggage. "The hot tubs have the greatest view of the mountains."

Something in the way he said it made Chiara think he had not spent time in those hot tubs alone. She would be perfectly happy to enjoy the hot tub in private, just as long as the water was hot and relaxed the muscles she knew she would be using for the first time in years.

The bellhop appeared, fussing with her suitcases. "Hello, Mr. Tanner," he said as he piled the cases onto a wheeled cart.

"How are you, Steve?" Curran stayed out of the bellhop's way as he rushed on to serve the next guest who pulled in behind them. Chiara retrieved her smaller bags, tucking them behind her before they disappeared from sight, too. Curran hesitated by his open car door. "Would you like me to stay and show you around?"

She considered it a moment, suddenly realizing she would be on her own here, no cast, no crew, for the first time in a while. But maybe she would be better off that way. Her trained senses would track the paranormal oddities that brought her here, and Curran's suspected ESP might do nothing but block her own perceptions. It was just after noon local time, and she had plenty of time to check things out before dark.

"How about tomorrow?" she asked, clutching her bag. "That way we can have breakfast, maybe, and plan a little."

He nodded with a little more enthusiasm. "Sounds like a date."

Her eyebrow shot up, her eyes wide as she stared at him, her heart taking an unusual few leaps. *Date? Who said anything about a date?* At the same time, some inner voice prodded her that she could do worse. He was nice looking, seemed well educated, and had polite connections to the locals. He could be useful to her.

Her reaction set him backpedaling. "Deal, I mean, great idea.

Nothing—nothing like that." He studied her for a long moment, and then waved to another car pulling up. "I'm in the way here today, and I'm sure you have work to do, settling in. I'll see you in the morning. About eight?"

"Sure, that's good." Unsure for just a moment whether she really wanted to be left alone in a strange part of the country, she inched toward the huge doors set into a heavy pine frame.

"See you then." He got back into his car and drove off. She watched until he disappeared down the long driveway, his presence still with her.

Once he was gone, she walked purposefully inside, finally claiming a portion of the special treatment she was used to. The Lodge's staff catered to her, sending her to the third floor balcony room with a welcome basket and a request to simply ask them for anything she needed. She found the room decorated with beautiful landscape paintings of Glacier's most memorable features, and the king size bed was spread in bright Native American designs. But nothing in the room compared with what she saw when she stepped out onto the redwood fenced balcony.

The mountain before her rose with the majesty of poetry to a snow capped peak far above her head. Another sat to the right, and another to its right, a perfectly sculptured range of mountains that looked like a cut from a nature documentary. The air smelled like pine and the wild flowers carpeting the ground below, including clumps of a tall white puffy flower she had never before seen. A raptor flew far overhead, joined by a second moments later. They cried out to each other, and then executed a graceful drive to the ground somewhere on the far side of the hotel.

Okay, so it wasn't Manhattan. The mountains were of rock instead of steel. And the city never smelled like this. Never.

Re-energized, she went inside and called the desk to hire a driver to take her out to the vortex. If the hotel was this inspiring, the psychic energy of this area might actually be amazing after all.

CHAPTER 7

MAX walked ahead of Astan and Elliun, taking a morsel of pride that he was chosen to be their lookout on their way to prepare the place of gathering. Daven Talvi would meet them there, to remove traces of the humans' passing, and then set certain magical wards in place to keep the area pure for the ceremony.

The temperature had steadily climbed since they had left the clan's forest bowers that morning, as it often did in the summer months, even on the mountain. All three elves had shed their early morning jackets, stashing them in a hollow tree along their path to be collected later. Their pace had been swift, a constant run since they had left the east side of the lake the humans called Flathead. Even little Elliun had kept up, another note of pride for Max. He must have trained him well.

Max stole a glance over his shoulder at his student, who puffed along, a little red faced. When he caught Max's eye, though, he straightened and fixed his eyes ahead on the pine lined path. Astan noticed, and nodded to Max.

"We'll stop after the crossing at the Feather Creek," he said.

Max acknowledged the order and then picked his way through some thorny underbrush to get them there. Astan swung Elliun up onto his shoulders so they could ford the creek quickly. Then the three of them hunkered down on a fallen log to have something to eat. Elliun handed out the leaf wrapped sandwiches his father had made, and they each had a spring apple. Fresh, cool water was in easy reach, so there was no reason to cart along a heavy canteen. When they had finished, Elliun inched away to explore the area, watching over his shoulder to see if anyone would stop him, but Astan did not seem concerned.

Astan did not seem concerned about a lot of things these days, a major change from the seasons past. His face was creased with smile lines, not worried wrinkles. The sight warmed Max's heart, and he felt he must comment on it.

"You seem happy," Max said.

Astan raised an eyebrow and then laughed. "I suppose I am. I have a wonderful mate, healthy children, all the woods I can walk in a day. Not because I'm in a position I ever thought I'd be in, that's for sure." He picked up a ragged piece of dead pine bark from the ground in front of them, sniffed it, and then studied its edges. "Life is all about the opportunities set in your path. Either you take advantage of them, or you lose out."

Wondering which of the many opportunities Astan referred to, Max opted to nod as if he understood. "The Circle has acknowledged Jelani's rule."

"Oh, that?" Astan chuckled and set the bark down. "Well, yes, they hadn't much other choice. Once she'd reunited the clan, and see even those who'd left years before returned to the fold, they had to acknowledge her." Astan's eyes shone with pride. "I still remember her face, that day when we all marched into Djana's little space, rebels and even humans in tow, and Jelani declared they were all our brothers and sisters. A small star glowed from within her. Who could deny that?"

Max grinned, remembering that day too, and how he had shown Lane the interconnections of the clan. "She has truly changed our future."

Astan leaned back, his hands on the log beside him. "Her example has shown us that in order to grow. We must all open up to possibilities of new things. The best example is her own birth. The great love her mother Linnea had for The Vincent, Jelani's human father, the Circle might have called it outrage at the time, and certainly it brought the clan through some horribly hard times when Bartolomey and the others refused to accept her. But if that love produced Jelani's brilliant determination and strength, a force that has continued to build power for our people over these last five years, then it has to be right. Just because something never happened before doesn't mean that it should be banned."

Max managed a small smile, considering what Astan said in light of his own history. "I am grateful that you see me in that same way."

They sat quietly for a moment as a pair of sleek gray water ouzels bickered, peeping and flapping over a part of the creek each wanted to claim as territory.

Astan laid a hand on Max's arm. "Jelani and I will never forget all you did when Elliun was under such threat. You were his guardian then, and you will always be."

"No matter what the Circle says?" Max could not help that last little quiver of insecurity in his voice.

Nothing in Astan's brown eyes spoke of deceit or betrayal, just pure honesty and respect. "No matter."

Max cocked his head, listening a moment for Elliun. The child was just out of sight in the direction of Goat's Peak, looking at something on his hands and knees. He was such a good boy, really. How could he be anything else with so many eyes watching him all the time?

"How are things going for you, Max? I see you've been in town. More shenanigans with Lane?"

Max chuckled. "The Lane has been very generous in his teaching of the games. Soon I will have all the powers of a Jedi knight."

"Really? A Jedi Knight?" Astan sounded impressed. "Is that...good?"

"Very good."

While Lane and his friends encouraged Max to continue to improve his scores in the game, and he had, he was disappointed that he had not been able to share Lane's success in transferring the skills and weapons acquired in the game into the real world. He read some of the books about Jedi knights and they clearly stated that young Jedi could build their own light sabers. But whenever he asked The Lane about it, he had just laughed and shook his head.

"You can't believe everything you read, pal," he said.

I know you brought Xiomar from your computer world into this one to help us bring down Bartolomey. Why can't I do the same thing? I'm the one with magic!

It did not make sense to him, not at all, and it niggled at the back of his mind, worst when he started feeling a little accomplished. It was as if he could not allow himself to just be proud of what he could do now. He felt he needed more.

What he required was one of those opportunities Astan was talking about. Given the right chance, he was sure he could become a super guardian. Then the Circle elders would never have to worry about the safety of Elliun or his family again.

The sun high overhead and Elliun feeling energized once again, Max sprang up from the log, walking over to retrieve the elf prince from his investigation. "Let's not keep your grandfather waiting!" And they were off again.

* * *

ANOTHER email arrived from the mysterious investigator, Miss DeLuna, indicating she had arrived in Montana, and this time Lane's personal paranoia alarm went off. The very pointed question she asked was: "I note that your fictional elves draw power from the earth in a magical way. Have you ever considered the possibility of writing them closer to the energy vortex?"

The implied, but unspoken corollary was, of course, *or is that where your elves get their power?*

And if that was the case, this Luna-tic was entirely too close to his clan.

The situation required a walk to the kitchen, a check of the refrigerator to find nothing particularly tasty waiting there, the preparation of a cup of tea, and about a five minute pacing session. After that, he fired back an overly polite response, asking her to meet with him at the coffee shop later that afternoon. He had to do something to sidetrack the woman, or at least convince her he was no expert.

What could he tell this Hollywood investigator to send her crawling back to whatever hole of a reality show people crawled out from?

He had written the story of how Jelani had found her family and rejuvenated the elf clan in a very real way, not so much in the 'no, but it really happened!' vein, but matter of factly. He had left out much of his own contribution to those events, preferring to keep the spotlight on the budding family and his Jelly Bean's amazing bravery to even consider such a life for herself. Fantasy was big in the indie press, and the book had found a certain niche, certainly enough so that he could afford guild dues for his online games and buy take out a couple times a week.

Lane never anticipated that someone would take this as serious research material.

Thank the Force I set it down in the Beaverhead-Deer Lodge forests near Butte and not here.

His computer beeped. She must have been sitting right on her laptop, because she accepted his invitation almost before he could close his browser. "Can't wait to meet such an accomplished writer!" She gushed.

"Oh, really," Lane muttered, knowing something was definitely wrong. "That's not what Mrs. Cowan always said in English class."

What was she really looking for? There was only one way to find out.

At the appointed time, still unsure of the direction he intended to steer this charlatan, he took the bus down to Higgins Avenue and made his way inside Butterfly Herbs. It was a busy afternoon, probably just about the three o'clock coffee break mark for the local workforce, and he was lucky to snag a corner booth by the back door just as a couple scooted out. It gave him a good place to sit with his back to the wall facing the door, so he could scope out the action.

A server he did not know came by to take his coffee order, and he settled for mountain blueberry scones since they did not carry Creamy Cupcakes. After she took his order, she returned to her position behind the counter, Lane scanned the shop. Memories flooded in of the years before when Jelani had worked as a barista here.

Back then he would come in once in awhile. Crispy's agoraphobia had paralyzed him to the point he would not go outside, and Lane had not liked leaving him alone for too long. Crispy's therapist, Iris was best friends with Jelani. When they discovered the mystery of Jelani's history and met her elven family members, Jelani left everything behind and moved up to the forest. Even then, she had craved Butterfly Herb's special chocolate hazelnut coffee. Whenever Lane would go to visit, he would faithfully stop to buy her a cup.

Those witches of the Circle actually believed the coffee made her have a son instead of a daughter! Talk about delusional.

"Mr. Donatelli?"

The well modulated voice, pitched in a golden honeyed tone, grabbed his attention, and he looked up to find the television diva standing before him. She had made some faux attempts to conceal herself, of course, the black brimmed hat with the lavender roses, the dark glasses, perhaps denim jeans just like everyone else in the coffee shop, but something about her silhouette shouted 'not of this place'. The other patrons seemed to catch. Most of them stared at her like she had dropped in from space.

"Uh, yeah, that's me," he said, struggling to heft his bulk off the booth bench, but she waved a hand at him.

"No, no, don't get up, that's fine." She slid in across from him and set her bright colored designer bag on the table. "I'm Chiara. I'm so glad you could meet with me."

The server brought his order and asked Chiara what she would like.

"Skinny latte with soy milk, no sugar." She eyed Lane's scones for a moment and then shook her head. "That's all."

The girl nodded and went to get her coffee. Lane studied the woman, sizing her up. *Let's start her a little off balance.*

"Why don't you just get water, if you're not getting real coffee?" he asked.

Her carefully colored pink lips pinched together a moment. "What do you mean?"

"Half the beauty of this place is that they grind their own beans, and the beans come in freshly roasted." Lane shrugged. "You'll never have coffee that tastes like this anywhere."

She hesitated a minute, and then gave a hint of a smile.

He stared at her dark glasses, wondering what she was hiding back there. She must have sensed his resistance, because she slid them off and set them on the table in front of her like a shield. Her eyes were a startling blue, and made up as if she were about to walk on camera.

What did she think this place was? The corner drug store where Betty Grable was discovered? Maybe some big movie director would come choose her as his next star? That look did not impress him.

He took a long sip of his coffee, thinking about what he wanted to say. Not much had come to him all afternoon, short of 'Go away!' The last avenue he had was the obvious one. "So you're investigating the vortex? Isn't that one of those places listed on the Weird and Wonderful Tourist Traps of America site? I'd hardly think it appropriate fodder for a program like yours."

A furrow graced her brow. After a moment, she chased it away with a determined smile. "Now, Mr. Donatelli—"

"You can call me Lane." His fat fingers reached for a scone, and he held it in one hand while tearing small bite sized pieces off it with the other, watching her watch him eat it as if she were starving. *Sucks to worry about those fifteen pounds the TV camera adds, huh?*

"Of course. Lane." She kept that smile on her face even as she thanked the girl for bringing her latte. "You've lived in this area long enough to know there's more to the energy vortex than just the buildings."

He fought to keep his gaze even into hers while his mind went crazy. What did she mean by that? What did she know about him? He had gone to great lengths to make sure no one would ever discover certain aspects of his past, even through an online search. Like his ghastly childhood, his stay in the foster care system, or his friend, Crispy. Before answering, he went for another gulp of coffee to wet his suddenly dry throat.

"Well, I've lived in Missoula for about ten years," he lied. "But the area you're talking about is nearly up to Glacier."

She reached in her purse and pulled out a small jeweled notepad and a purple pen. "But you write about it with such authority."

She didn't challenge me. She doesn't really know. The realization calmed his racing heart. *She's fishing, that's all. I hope.*

He finished his scone and then laughed. "I write about life on Coruscant with authority too, but it doesn't mean I've been there."

She did not even register a note of interest in the name, which brought him an internal snicker. She really did not know much about the geek culture. For once, perhaps he had the upper hand in this battle of wits. A tiny voice in his head whispered: *Inconceivable.* He mentally slapped it down.

She consulted a small writing pad of notes, something tall, narrow and floral, covered by scribbles in purple ink. "But your elves live in harmony with the earth, drawing energy from it. A...symbiosis of sorts, isn't it?"

"Sure. You know, if you read Native American legends around here, you'll see the exact same thing. The Kootenai, the Flathead Salish, all those children of the earth." He hoped he did not sound too condescending, but she was a cool customer, and definitely hard to read.

She scribbled a few words on her pad. "The clan, you said, is ruled by a queen and a circle of elders? Now, how do they get this energy from the earth, exactly? Do they just absorb it through their feet? Do they even wear shoes? Or do they have to enchant it from the earth by rituals?"

Much, much too close. The entertainment value of teasing her suddenly dried up. "Look, Chiara, you realize that my book is a work of fiction, right? You understand the concept of fiction. As in 'something I made up'? Not real?"

She smiled at him, and a shadow like a spider in her web

hung in that curve of her lip. "I'm sure you're saying so now."

"You're effing delusional, that's what's wrong with you." Lane leaned as close to the table as he could get, his generous paunch in the way. Chiara was not the only one who did investigations.

"You see things that aren't there. That's why that amusement park haunting was a bust. Why you couldn't find a speck of alien dust in that mountain community near Asheville. And have you already forgotten that ghostly schoolgirl roaming the halls of that tornado destroyed town? Oh wait. We never saw her on your show. Because she didn't exist."

Each example he gave ripped some support out of that smarmy grin, and her eyes grew wider, and when he finished, the pen slipped from her fingers. She looked like a different person. Maybe even someone real. The difference surprised him.

He opened his mouth to speak again, but she recovered before he could say anything. She became a whirl of motion, shoving her pad back into her purse, pushing herself out of the booth, hardly stopping to say goodbye before she careened through the crowded shop and out the front door, leaving the patrons again staring after her.

The girl who waited on them came back over, eyeing the half full latte cup. "Is everything all right?"

Lane ate the last bite of his scone, not sure if he felt proud of his effort or not. "I sure hope so," he said.

"You're paying for her coffee?"

"Sure, why not?" He dug in his pocket and gave the girl a ten. Maybe he got screwed, or maybe it assuaged his conscience a little. The important thing now was to hightail it north and let Jelani know how much crazy was headed her way.

CHAPTER 8

THE ethereal 'room' where the elves' Circle met was packed with the curious and the necessary after Lane and Crispy arrived at the clan's lands. Crispy disappeared into the woods with Max and Elliun, since crowds were never his thing. Lane, however, got pushed front and center of the gathering, to share the news about Chiara DeLuna's intentions.

Jelani stood with him, as did Daven Talvi. The buzz of the gathered faded to an electric hum when Jelani spoke sharply across the chatter. "I don't think this will matter to us, but I'd like some input from you all," she said. "Go ahead, Lane."

Lane gave a nervous cough, though his trust level had grown since the days he was always on the fence about whether the old elf ladies would turn him into a newt. He was a mage of the clan now, his stripes earned in that final battle with Bartolomey. They needed him to balance the power structure in their clan. But they could be whacky. And you could never quite trust whacky.

"I've been contacted by a television reporter about the vortex," he began. "Uh…how many of you remember what television is?"

Djana eyed him from her usual seat square in the middle of the front row, on a polished portion of a fallen fir's trunk. "Another human abomination," she grumbled.

"Yeah, thanks so much for the vote of confidence, Grams." Lane could not keep the note of sarcasm from his voice. "Don't forget humans invented the device that finally got rid of old Black Bart, huh?"

Daven smiled and touched Lane's arm. "I think she gets your point. Let's move on."

"Right. So she's one of these people who goes around stirring up and supposedly debunking claims of ghosts, magic, and paranormal phenomena. She's currently got her eye set on your vortex, and not just like one of the regular tourists, either. She'll bring in a camera crew and film it and try to prove its magic or call it a fake."

Djana had not given up. "How is it that you know about her coming?"

"She contacted me because of the book," Lane explained. "For some reason, she thinks I'm some sort of expert."

"The book that we advised against you writing?" Djana asked.

Lane could swear he felt the pricking of a handful of pine needles on the back of his neck at the disapproval in her voice. "Yeah, actually, I think it was that one." He cleared his throat. "The more important part is that she's here, now, and she intends to scope out the vortex this week."

A collective gasp swept through those gathered, perhaps thirty or more, like a mountain wind. So it really was as bad as he suspected. "When exactly is the clan ritual going to be?"

Eyes closed, Jelani cocked her head as if she were calculating. "The night of the solstice is June 21. Four days from now."

Lane nodded. "Maybe she'll be done by then. I'm thinking once she gets to the site and talks with the folks at the cabin, she'll get her filming done there and not look any farther. She doesn't seem the type who likes to go tromping around in the woods."

But then neither am I, and I'm sure as heck here.

Daven agreed. "Often humans have no real interest in what is not directly before them, no offense intended to our human guests, but it is true. Our ceremony takes place a slight distance away from the human commemorative site, so we may safely suspect she will not have any reason to look further into the outlying portions of the land."

Lane wrestled with how much else to tell them, partly because of the hostility Djana had already shown about his book. If he had thought anyone would have taken the damned thing seriously, he would never have put it on paper. He finally erred on the side of more information being better than less and prepared to duck.

"There's more. She started asking me questions about the elves in the book, how the energy is transferred from them to the earth and re-absorbed. She even wanted to know if elves wear shoes, so they can touch the earth directly. I did what I could to redirect her. But it's going to be touch and go. You're not going to want to reveal anything to her production company, if you don't want to be exposed at all."

By their sudden silence, he knew they were beginning to realize the depth of the problem.

Jelani paced across the front of the gently walled room, her head bowed in thought. "We cannot move the ritual. It must occur on the solstice. Perhaps we could create a bower around the site?" For this, she looked to the Circle.

Daven jumped in on that, too. "The mages will need to confer, to decide what we can do to protect the ritual from prying eyes. Perhaps there is some diversion magic to ward attention away."

"It would be best if this woman were sent away altogether," Djana said. "What are the possibilities of such a thing?"

Astan's friend Beckley, a blond, broad shouldered elf, spoke up from the back of the room. "We could set up a perimeter of guards, instructing them to create magic distractions, to draw her away from the area of the ritual."

Lane shook his head. "No, no. You don't want to give her anything she can use as fuel for this investigation. Anything 'spooky' or 'magic' or even the least bit interesting and out of the ordinary will convince her there's something here worth her time." He shifted his weight onto the other leg, wishing he had thought to bring his own chair. Those logs were hard on his hind end, which is why he was standing now.

"Even if you get through the ritual safely, she'll be sniffing around for something to show her viewers. Heck, maybe we can find Bigfoot and send her trailing after him. Anyone know where to find him?"

A roomful of stares, and Beckley finally laughed. "Nice try,

Lane, but we will not sacrifice the other residents of the forest to save ourselves."

A beat of silence followed, and Lane looked up sharply. He had been kidding, but Beckley's expression was dead serious. *Really? Bigfoot?*

Jelani stopped in front of him. "How determined will she be to find something?"

Lane shrugged. "From what I've seen in gossip and rumor on the Internet, she's at risk of losing her show and being discredited entirely. She's not going to give up until she finds something."

"We'll have to think about this. But yes, at the very least, I want the Circle and mages to create a bower around the ritual area. That should be able at least to protect us during the ritual. Once we get through that, we can plan to stay at home. Or even take time in the western parts of our lands until this woman loses interest."

"Whatever you say, Jelly Bean."

She hugged him, giving him warm fuzzies right down to his toes. "Thanks for coming up here to tell us about this. It's important that we knew."

"No prob. Let me know if you need something else." Lane gathered up his stuff to go, noting that Daven came outside with him, while Jelani communed some more with the witches. *What's up with Papa Bear now?*

"I thought we might speak of the ritual and what your part could be," Daven said as they walked the path toward Jelani's tree house.

Even after five years of living in the woods, Jelani still had not chosen one of the magic woven bowers as her home. Instead she remained in the tree house Daven had created for her when she first came to the forest. Lane did not understand the magic behind it, particularly when Daven expanded it with each child Jelani birthed. It was now bigger than his and Crispy's apartment, but only on the inside. The outside looked just like any other big old tree trunk.

"Yeah, I was wondering about that myself. Not too much call

for computer programming in this energy twister thingy."

Daven's warm laugh brought a rush of heat to Lane's face. *Why does he always make me feel like an idiot?*

"The energy source is one with the earth, Lane. While it flows everywhere, even here, the strength fluxes, as scientists say, with time and place. The forces of the solstice concentrate the flow around the vortex, making it much easier to access. You've felt it, we all have. You're right, it's not something you make happen, it's something that happens as part of our natural world."

"But Jelly Bean said that it's acting in an unnatural way."

"True. We will need to use all the forces at our disposal at that time to concentrate and restructure the flow."

"So what do you need a computer nerd for?"

Daven grinned. "It is not your technical skills that we need, young Jedi." He winked and Lane bit his tongue before ordering the mage out of his head. "Your heart holds a place for humankind in the balance of the solstice."

Lane felt his cheeks get hot and tried like hell not to be embarrassed. "All right. I can buy that."

"Bring Crispy, as well. The calming forces of the *Donoma* will help him." Daven hesitated. "He begins to have troubled thoughts once more."

"Yeah, as a matter of fact he has. How do you know?"

"What is it you humans say? A magician never divulges his secrets?"

Daven's light laugh did not reassure Lane in the least. "He's started to pull back in that shell. He even quit going out to the animal rehab place."

"Have you spoken with Iris?"

"Iris has so much to do now, between her time up here and what time she has in town. I didn't want to bother her. And Crispy definitely didn't want to talk about it." He leaned against a thick tree trunk and sighed. "I was hoping it was just a seasonal affect thing, or a funk of some sort, and he'd get over it."

"When did that start? Was there something that triggered it?"

Lane thought back. "Right about the beginning of May. He

and some of the elf kids spent the day in the forest by that old spot where the monkey wrenching was going on, you know, where Black Bart grabbed Jelani and Astan thought you were shot and all that? When Crispy came home, he was real quiet, and then this started."

Staring off into the distance, Daven almost seemed to travel away from Lane. "His heart is filled with sorrow. Something still binds him to the past."

"Something? Like what? Iris said he'd put the abuse behind him. Both of us have, Iris said so."

"Tell me about that spot. What connections does it have for him?"

"That spot? Oh, man. That's where we ended up when you all were up there. Astan hauled you back to the cabin after one of Bart's guys shot you. There was this creepy elf that kind of mind effed all of us. Even Astan was frozen. But not Crisp. He went ape shit. He killed the guy with his bare hands. I guess he thought it was Sammy's step dad."

Lane tried to ignore the worm of nausea that slid through his stomach at the memory of their thin, bruised foster brother. When Sammy was not being sent back to his mom and her abusive boyfriend for 'trial' visits, Crispy had become particularly close to him. The last visit Sammy did not come back. The boyfriend 'accidentally' beat him to death.

And Crispy had gotten revenge for poor Sammy, in his own way. "Oh, maybe that's it. Sammy."

"Yes," Daven said. "That hurt from the past is tied to his remorse for what happened that day."

"He must have been able to sublimate it for a while, once he'd recovered and became free to go outside and all. But now things have died down."

A ribbon of worry crossed Daven's forehead. "Sublimate it? As in hide it away?"

"Yeah?" Something in Daven's tone flagged the crazy meter in Lane's consciousness. "All right. What did you do?"

Daven back pedaled. "Why do you assume I have *done*

something?" When Lane just stared, Daven's lips set in a hard line. "Perhaps I did."

Lane waited for several long minutes, but when Daven was not forthcoming, he smacked his forehead. "Don't make me drag it out of you, Daven. What happened? And how are we going to fix it?"

"I must speak to Iris. I *helped* him move past what happened the day we rescued Linnea." He crossed his arms. "Perhaps I should have let him recover on his own."

Lane scowled. "So you buried it, and it's finding its way out again."

"It is natural that the cycle would come around once again. Perhaps I should speak with him. Or Iris." He smiled. "She remains very fond of you both. She would be concerned."

"Yeah, he might come out for her."

"Good. Then we will expect you both at the ritual, without your new found media friend."

"Oh, you can count on that. I have no intention of bringing that one out here. No, thank you. She's going to have to handle this investigation on her own."

Daven nodded and patted his shoulder. Lane did not pull away, as much as he wanted to, his body resonating with *don't whammy me!* As far as he could tell, the mage left him intact, although with a little buzz of well being that warmed him through like a fuzzy blanket. *As much as I want to hate that guy sometimes, he always finds a way to make me feel better. Damn him.*

"Be well," Daven said, and he turned to go back into the bower.

Lane trundled off to find where he had parked the truck, his mind already scrabbling out ways to convince Crispy to come up with him to the ceremony.

Hey, if they can recharge their clan and give Crisp a reboot as well, it was all good.

CHAPTER 9

CHIARA'S retreat to her hotel after her encounter with that fat oaf seemed more shameful than it really was, she realized as she pulled into the parking lot. All the way back from Missoula she chided herself about trying to connect with the locals, especially someone who seemed as ignorant as Lane Donatelli.

His words had stung her, there was no doubt. The smudged mascara under her eyes told her that, though she refused to admit that he had really made her cry. She doubted everything, especially herself at this point. She did not need help from some computer fattened geek slob. Even if something in his eyes told her he knew a whole lot more than he was saying. At least no one else had heard what he said. Her shame was limited.

Now that she was finished with him, she could get back to the woods and her work. She had made a couple of ventures into the forest, hiking by herself gingerly through the wild growth, glad no one could see her. She had not found much. *That just means I have to keep digging.*

She checked in at the desk for messages, since she left her information with Janie back in New York. Maybe Hunter had rethought his harsh words. Perhaps he even sent her a vase of lilacs, wanting to make things up to her.

But there was nothing. No one cared.

Her phone rang before she could get out of the elevator, and she grabbed it, glad of the distraction. "Chiara DeLuna," she said, in as pleasant a voice as she could muster.

"Chiara, it's Curran Tanner. I'm sorry to call so soon after we parted this morning, but I wondered if we might have a chance to take a run out to the Yaak today."

She rolled her eyes. What was up with the guy? Was he a secret agent for the local Chamber of Commerce? He knew she was a paranormal investigator, not a host on the Travel Channel. "Look, we had a nice breakfast, Curran, but I'm on a timetable here. I wanted to hit the vortex site again, check lighting and so on before the crew gets here."

There was a long pause on the other end of the phone. "That's a shame. I hoped I'd get to see you again."

Something in his voice indicated honest disappointment and longing, not a pitch. The realization caught her up short. He really wanted to be with her? Not her public persona, just her?

Take that, Hunter Nowles.

Needing that particular sort of ego boost, she reconsidered her excuse. "You know what, Curran? I think I do have some time about mid-afternoon. We'd be back by sunset? I really want to see what the site's like in half light."

His voice brightened immediately. "Sure thing. I promise. I'll drive you there myself."

And no cost out of her pocket for gas. Maybe she could even wangle a meal out of it too. She hated thinking that way, but with her show and possibly her future on the line, she might have to start watching every single dime. Chiara liked to live much too large to do that.

"Great. I'll see you soon then."

Action, that's what she needed. Some forward motion. She marched down the hall to her room and opened the door, keenly aware of the king sized pillow top bed, the Jacuzzi tub and the other perks that came with being 'Chiara'. She could do this. She could do anything. She had been on her own since her mother died, except for her odd maiden aunt who had never really known what to do with a teenaged budding psychic. Aunt Shariah never did understand the gift, and mostly just let Bonnie run about on her own as long as the police did not call to complain.

Once inside, she hurried to the bathroom to repair her face. A good scrub made her feel a bit more human. She shrugged off the dark sweater she had worn to impress Lane Donatelli, for all the good that had done, and flipped through the hangers in her closet, looking for something that was a little more flirty. *But remember we're going tramping around some muddy river.* She pursed her lips with displeasure as she thought about ruining her boots. *Well hellfire, as my old grandfather would have said, they're boots. That's what they're for.*

Her grandfather, of course, would have had a pair of hard working leather steel toed boots, not the dainty things Chiara had found so darling on a site online for half a week's paycheck.

Half an hour later, when Cullen called up from the lobby, she was attired in a faux fur trimmed sky blue winter coat and a lined pair of new denim jeans, and her designer boots with three inch heels. Her cheeks were pink with anticipation, and gold earrings dangled attractively from her ears. She read in his face how good she looked. *Wonderful.*

He held the door as she climbed into his sports utility vehicle, and then came around to the driver's side. "Beautiful day for a drive," he said. She noticed how his eyes sparkled, his smile delighted, and she felt like all that enthusiasm was for her alone. *How long had it been since Hunter had been so expressive?* She tried not to remember.

She had never driven through the Montana backwoods, and the beauty of it took her breath away. Around each corner appeared a vista that demanded recording before it vanished. The mountains rose, dark against a blue sky, many still snow topped, their wrap of evergreens trailing up their sides to the summit. They alternated with valleys plunged in greens and bluest of blue lakes, in between the two, fields of peacefully grazing animals and other signs of daily life. All the time she was aware of that wide open sky.

She thought the term *Big Sky Country* was merely something advertisers coined to sell the region. Like *The Big Apple* for New York. But seeing it for herself, she had to admit it was true. The blue expanse of sky seemed to go on forever.

The river itself had multiple personalities, portions of it flat and calm, other parts full and rushing over the rocks between its banks. They drove for about fifteen minutes after first spotting it. Then Curran parked his vehicle and came around to open her door. She stepped down onto the grass, trying not to let her mouth gape open at the view.

"See, I knew you'd like it," he said. "Come on, let's get a closer look."

She would have been perfectly satisfied to remain right where she was, but Curran took her hand, and held it tight, not letting her weasel out of the walk. All she could think as she inched down the side of the bank was that if she died because of the damned boots, at least no one had a video camera.

"Spectacular, isn't it?" he asked. "My granddad used to bring me fishing up here."

"Fishing, really?" She stared down at the water, not having really considered the possibility of live animals in there.

"Sure." He made sure she was safe on the bank and then skimmed a large flat rock across the top of the water. It crossed completely to the other side. She suspected it was not the first time he had done it. "Lot of good trout in here. Occasionally a salmon, but we usually go over to Idaho to get those."

"Oh," she replied, trying to sound as if she knew that already. She glanced sideways at him to see if he was judging her ignorance, but he seemed perfectly absorbed in the process of finding more rocks to skip. Relieved, she turned her attention to the sights and sounds of the river. She guessed the middle of the expanse of water might be six to eight feet deep, but the shallows led a good portion of the way in. "It's not very deep."

Curran laughed. "If I had my boots, I'd be out there." He drew a finger across his leg just short of his hip.

"Those big boots? I've seen pictures of them." She inched closer to the water. "Do you have to wear those if you want to fish here?"

"Only if we go out into the water. No reason why we can't fish from the bank, and honestly, it scares away less fish." He broke into a smile. "But sometimes you just want to be part of the river itself."

"So what's all that waving of the pole for? I haven't noticed many bugs at all."

He stared at her blankly and then shrugged off her words. "We're not waving the pole. That's the point of fly fishing. You create these little lures, or flies, out of feathers and other things, and you use it like bait to entice the fish. Because it's not alive, it doesn't wiggle in the water like a worm on a hook. In order to attract a fish, it needs to be kept moving, lighting on the top of the water, like a real insect would do."

She mentally pictured that for a moment, and adjusted that picture until it made sense.

"It's all in the wrist." He demonstrated holding an imaginary rod and flicking the tip out and back with incredible ease. She could see he had a lot of practice.

"Caught one of my biggest rainbow trout ever right south of here before the falls," he said. He held his hands about eighteen inches apart. "Cleaned it and ate it before we left the river. Better than any you've had in your big city, I bet."

"Well, I don't know," she began, but then she cut off the brag about her last visit to Ocean House. Maybe Curran was right. Who was she to dispute him on a point she really did not know anything about?

"If you're around long enough, maybe I'll be able to show you," he said. "I've got plenty of fishing equipment. You won't have to tie your own flies, not unless you want to learn." He seemed plenty eager to teach her, if she did.

She allowed a small smile, not wanting to promise anything she was not sure she could deliver. After all, the point in being here was to get her story, wrap it up on film, and get back to New York in hopes of redeeming herself. Right?

But watching Curran delight in the rolling passage of the small, foamy rapids like he was a small boy, she found herself enjoying the view. She had several weeks before her feature was due. Maybe she should make the effort to stop and smell the pine needles.

CHAPTER 10

BECKLEY and some of the Youngers conferred about the problem and, for the first time, invited Max to their council.

He was honored. The group stopped about halfway up the mountain which the humans named Strawberry Mountain. In case his invitation had been a mistake, Max stayed to the edge of the group hoping not to be noticed. But Beckley grinned and called him forward.

"No, brother, your days of sneaking about eavesdropping are over. You're too important not to know what's going on, and helping out if you can."

Embarrassed at the sudden attention, Max took the indicated seat, stealing a look around at the others to see if they approved. Some seemed to. Others ignored both Max and Beckley, more interested in little squabbles between themselves, which seemed to be attuned to the seating or positions of honor in the upcoming ritual.

Perhaps Max was young and naïve about such things, but he could not believe what he was hearing. *Had the Youngers learned nothing? Was there always to be political discontent among the clan?*

Max pursed his lips, annoyed, drawing a chuckle from Vez, seated to his right.

"What troubles you, friend? Young *nians* will always be so."

Max eyed Vez a moment, very aware that Vez himself had once been a malcontent, to the point he had attacked Jelani and attempted to steal Elliun away. Astan, Jelani and Beckley might have forgiven Vez, knowing he was under the influence of the mage Veraena. But Max found it hard to let the past go so easily. "Perhaps you were," he replied to Vez. "I was not."

Vez pulled back, his eyes wide for moment. Then he nodded. "It is true. You have always been loyal to the clan."

Max nodded. "The clan has fed me and cared for me through the years, as a mother and father would have done. I can do no less."

Vez appeared thoughtful. "Yet they have never treated you as an equal."

Max shrugged. It was an obvious statement, requiring no response.

"But you still devote yourself fully to the queen and her consort."

Max frowned, uncomfortable with his companion's words. Why should he not follow the leaders of the clan? Was Vez trying to incite sedition? "Of course. They believe in me."

Fontine leaned around Vez's shoulder with a little wag of her finger. "Vez, leave him be. Once you were accepted back into the clan, you know how much you needed that welcome and support. We're so much stronger now, all of us, together." She smiled, a dimple coming into her left cheek, including Max in her warmth.

Vez grinned and caught her finger, pulling her hand to his lips to kiss it. "I mean no harm, my lady."

Fontine laughed and sat down on the tree trunk next to him, still smiling as Vez leaned close and whispered in her ear.

Relieved that Vez's attention had been diverted, Max felt a small pang of jealousy at their obvious intimacy. He might be small, his build more conducive to his gifts than normal growth would have been, but he and Vez were of an age. Max noticed the young *neris* of the clan, considered their varied appeal, and wished he had one who looked at him the way Fontine looked at Vez. But none would. They still considered him a child.

Looking out over the valley below, Max appreciated the clear view. The winter snows and spring rains past, the warm season had arrived, the clouds white as a fawn's underbelly, and the sky a brilliant blue. In the distance, the clouds kissed the tops of the mountains, but that was far away. Today the weather would be the kind that brought fresh breath to the lungs and an extra spring to the step. Even for those who were no longer children.

Max noted belatedly that none of Jelani's family were present.

Astan often hunted and held counsel with the Youngers, as he had growing up. It seemed strange that he would not be included here.

Perhaps that is why I have been invited, to stand as his proxy in this mysterious matter.

When all had been seated, Beckley spoke. "The threat from the outside world has grown closer for years as the humans expand their reach into the lands that have traditionally been of use to us. But we are faced with a different sort of danger now, with the intrusion of this media woman. I believe what Lane says about her. She is ruthless in pursuit of her goal, and she will not stop until she succeeds."

"But I thought he said she simply investigates the human access to the Vortex in the town, not our *Donoma*.," Amin said. "Why should this concern us? Humans have been in the town for many years, studying the effects of the energy field in that enclosure. Surely this is nothing new."

"That's *not* all she's doing," Elron said, standing up to garner everyone's attention. His tall, spare frame stretched taut with tension, even his brow wrinkled with worry. "The hawks follow her, and she's gone into the forest all around the human habitations. She's come close to the river several times."

Elron's gift was the ability to communicate with and control all the birds of the air, so Max knew if the hawks had found her where she should not be, Elron would report it accurately. His mind pictured the spot on the riverbank where he, Daven and Astan had cleared the area of all loose stones and sticks, ready for the clan to gather for the ritual. Had the human woman noticed their preparations? Would that pique her interest even more? A cold chill passed through his midsection.

"Isn't this a problem for the mages? Or the queen?" asked Terzon as he leaned lazily against a tree trunk. "Why haven't they taken action? Why should we concern ourselves, when we have our own pursuits to call us?"

Max eyed the dark haired *nian* with suspicion. Terzon had come back from the failed rebellion without family connections to welcome him, as did Vez. He remained prickly, but in a controlled way, skirting the displeasure of the Circle and those who ruled. "This trouble belongs to us all," Max muttered.

"Exactly," Beckley said, with a nod in Max's direction. "Lane says the woman is desperate to achieve her personal fame through this discovery. We all know desperate people do dangerous things." He set his farseeing gaze square on Terzon's face. Terzon's jaw set, but he did not look away.

"Astan is aware of these things," Beckley went on. "He and Daven seem more immediately worried about the instability of the *Donoma* and the ritual that will hopefully heal it. The queen is only concerned about the health of the clan, and how the *Donoma* will affect the living beings under its influence."

Fontine spoke quietly from her seat beside Vez. "We cannot expect the queen and the mages to tend to us like we are children. They have larger responsibilities."

Terzon grumbled, and Beckley spoke louder to cover his complaints. "Astan believes that the woman is more of an annoyance than a true menace. I am not sure I agree. Lane understands this kind of thing better than we can. If he believes there's potential danger in this investigation, I'm going to stand with him, as he stood with us against Bartolomey. As odd as he is, he still seems to have our best interests at heart."

Max felt compelled to defend any implied insult to his friend. "The Lane is our representative mage, as well. He is bound by magic to us. He would not lead us in a false path!"

A commotion broke out in the back, with a mocking tone. Max could not see who spoke, but it was clear to him that whoever it was not only denigrated Lane but also Max himself. He got to his feet to challenge the one who had impugned his honor, but Beckley cut off discussion with a sharp tongue.

"*I* lead the Youngers, and *I* say what we're going to do. Until the woman poses an open threat to us, we will take no overt action against her. But we will spend the time between now and the high ritual combing the forests, watching this woman and her crew every moment."

Terzon scowled. "Watching? Really? That's all?"

Beckley turned to Max. "What does the queen say about her?"

Max shrugged. "That she'll likely stay on her side of the line. As long as she does, then there's no problem."

Beckley's lips curved into a slight smile. "Then it would seem our orders would be to 'keep her on her side of the line.' That seems to give us as much leeway as we need. We do that, whatever it takes."

A rumble of voices, more enthusiastic this time, passed through those gathered like a wind blown wave on the lake. "More like it!" someone called.

Terzon stood up with a few of his new cronies, making their way to the front. "We'll take first watch."

Beckley eyed them a long moment. Then he nodded. "We must patrol many areas of territory from the place where she is staying at the lodge, to the energy field. We need more teams. Maybe six or seven. She cannot be allowed to discover the truth of the *Donoma*."

He assigned several more small groups, who banded up and headed out. When Max would have volunteered, Beckley refused.

"You have more important duties. My friend. The prince is in your care. Of all things, he should not come to the attention of outside forces."

"Of course not." Stung by Beckley's reminder, Max stood up and crossed his arms. "I know what is expected of me, and I will do it."

Beckley clapped him gently on the shoulder. "I never doubted that, Max, or your bravery. Let the others take care of this, while you pursue your own duties. If you need anything, let me know."

Max left the meeting feeling a bit disloyal, almost like he was sneaking around behind Jelani's back. He could have told her what Beckley had done. No one had forbid him to do so. But he understood that the Youngers had done this in an effort to help the queen and the others prepare by relieving the burden on their shoulders. The Youngers could handle this. It was also likely that without the necessity of the Circle's oversight, they would actually be more effective.

But he should have known nothing was as simple as it seemed. Word got around, as it always did, and Elliun's little ears burned with the excitement of it all.

"So are we going to see them?" Elliun scarcely waited until they had cleared the door of the tree house before he grabbed Max's arm, excitement emanating from him like moon glow through fog. "Those people Lane said? The spooky woman?"

Max pressed his lips together in the way he had seen Djana do when extremely adamant. He imagined that scowling face to give himself a little more backbone. He knew Jelani and Astan would not approve of Elliun exposing himself to the human media culture.

Even if he himself was avidly curious, especially since Beckley had excluded him almost pointedly from the group effort.

"Those who have the gifts will deal with this situation, Elliun." He led the way along a trail to the east, distracted by a nest of small rabbits that scattered in their path, stirring up dried, crackly leaves that remained from the winter before. When Elliun would have chased after them, Max drew him back to their appointed plan. "We've got to scout the Ocona range by nightfall, Elliun. We can't get there and back if we let our intentions wander."

The prince stomped along behind him, radiating unhappiness, sullen disappointment written on his face. Max tried to hide his smile at Elliun's petulant efforts to prolong the disagreement. *Were all young children this expressive without saying a word?* He did not think so. From what he remembered of his own youth, at this age he spent a lot of time trying not to be noticed at all. So often coming to someone's attention meant being ridiculed or reminded of his differences.

Not anymore.

But he remembered how it felt to be excluded, left out of the plans and purposeful action of the others. It hurt. The last thing he wanted was to make Elliun feel the same way.

"Don't worry, Elliun. I'm sure if they find something we can contribute, they won't hesitate to ask."

The response perked the boy up and he ran to walk alongside his mentor as they reached the first steep climb they had to make. "I could make her go away," Elliun said, with the matter of fact confidence of a young child.

Max paused in his light ascent of the rock wall before them. "How would you do that?"

Elliun smiled mysteriously. "Magic."

"Magic." The facile answer left Max unimpressed, and he resumed the climb. "What kind of magic do you think would make her go away?"

Elliun cocked his head. "Mostly charm. Like The Lane."

Max laughed and held out a hand to haul his young charge to the top. "It's true, the Lane can talk his way out of just about any situation. But even he has been powerless against this human investigator."

Lane had not been specific what wiles the woman had used, but something in the aura he gave off when speaking of her conveyed to Max the depth of his disturbance.

But Elliun was not prepared to surrender so easily. "Mother is half human, isn't she? Grandfather was human? Why is this woman so evil?"

He scrambled on top of the rock, sitting down, cross legged, in a stance Max recognized as 'planting'. When the young prince did this, it was likely he would not move again until he had received a satisfactory answer. Elliun had his share of the queen's stubborn temper.

Max hesitated, torn between just closing the door on this issue, which was clearly beyond the scope of what Elliun needed to concern himself with, and wanting to encourage the boy's curiosity. "She's not evil, Elliun. Not like Bartolomey or those who would overthrow our leaders. She's like a child running carelessly through the forest that crushes plants and disturbs wildlife. She would thoughtlessly cause harm to the clan."

Elliun cocked his head. "If she is like a child, that means she needs to be taught."

Wherever this was going, Max did not like it. This child had no business instructing dangerous humans. He changed the subject. "And so do you, which is why we are out in the forest today. Come on." He turned his back on the child and started walking away, half convinced Elliun would not follow. But to Max's surprise, he did.

The two walked through knee high brush, on route to a spot in the woods Max knew to be full of wildlife. He glanced behind, pleased to note that their passage was invisible. Elves' innate abilities included an altered sense of gravity. When Elliun was old enough to train at combat, he would learn, as they all did, how to adjust his weight to his advantage in battle, making himself lighter or heavier as need dictated. But moving through the grasses or even along a muddy shoreline, their steps should not be seen after their passing.

Not so with the animals of the forest, however, and this was the subject of today's lesson. When Max reached the edge of a familiar clearing, he paused and hunkered down behind a thick fir trunk. Elliun crouched down, creeping up beside him. The two waited for many long seconds, Max visually scanning the area for potential lesson pointers. The younger elf waited patiently for a short while, and then began to fidget.

"What are we doing here?" he whispered.

Max listened for a few more seconds, and then turned to face his young pupil. "Elliun, there have been no less than ten animals of various kinds within the length of a tall tree from this place this morning. I want you to identify and locate them."

Elliun's dark eyes opened wide. "Ten? Are you sure?" A hint of dismay in his tone, he stretched up just a little, to see over the fallen trunk that lay between them and the clearing. "I can't see anything at all."

Max nodded. "Probably not from there."

Elliun shot him a look and then inched forward over the trunk, staying low to the earth as Max had previously instructed.

His gaze first fanned over the open ground, where Max had noted both scat and footprints before he settled into his hiding place. As he approached the prints, a flutter of large wings overhead caught his attention, just as the white speckled brown underside of a Coopers hawk burst from the branches and shot skyward with a flip of its long tail, accompanied by its usual sound when alarmed, a strident *cak-cak-cak*. Though the bird never dipped into the clearing at all, the startled Elliun ducked nearly flat and Max had to smile.

Recovering himself, Elliun sat up, holding one finger in the air until Max nodded. *Nine to go.*

Shifting his attention to the prints in the ground, Elliun studied them long enough that Max finally made his way into the clearing. "Claws," Elliun said, pointing out indentations above the toe pads. "A wolf?"

Max nodded. "Can you see how long ago?"

Elliun looked at the area around the tracks, searching for more clues. He then closed his eyes. When he opened them again, he looked right into Max's face. "About ten minutes. Then she went off to the east."

"How do you know that?"

"I just know."

Elliun stood up and walked in the direction he said the wolf had gone. Just outside the clearing he bent down, indicating a pile of scat. "She was here."

Max bit his lip, knowing Elliun had, through his genetics, special gifts that likely showed him such things in a way that was much easier than other elves like himself had to use, the tried and true examination of the scat for hair and bone residue, indicating a carnivore, rather than seeds or leaves, which would be a plant eater, its size telling whether it was a small or large animal, the moisture content revealing clues to how long since it had been dropped. This pile was in fact moist, so Elliun was clearly correct. It just seemed like he had shortcut the learning process using his mother's, or perhaps his grandfather's, intuition about the natural world.

Another way Max fell short of the skills of other elves. This was not one of his talents. *That just means I have shall try harder to teach him.*

"Looks like you're right. What else?"

Elliun stood up and cocked his head, listening. "Bees. In a hive. Over there." He pointed up into the trees. Max had found the hive weeks earlier when he and some of the Youngers had been searching for honey, so he knew Elliun was correct.

"Very good."

Elliun walked around the edge of the clearing checking the tree trunks. He tapped one as he went by and a clutch of squirrels scattered into the upper branches, making him laugh. "That would be seven," he said.

He stopped in front of one tree trunk, finding long scratches on it at a place about the height of a grown elf. The top layers of bark had also been peeled away, leaving shredded edges. Max knew what that meant. Did his pupil?

About to speak, Elliun froze a moment. "Shh," he said, holding up his right hand.

Rustling came in the woods directly behind Max, something large. Remembering the days of clan war, he spun around, placing himself between Elliun and whatever approached. But it was no elf, hostile or otherwise. A ten point buck entered the clearing, closely followed by two does. They stopped when they realized the elves were there, and then the deer bolted off to the west.

"That's three," Elliun cackled. "Ten. Just like you said."

Max grinned. "You amaze me."

Elliun's smile faded a little. "But I can't fly."

Max slipped an arm around the younger elf's shoulders, pleased that he would acknowledge some special capability that Max did have. "Not yet, anyway. The teacher is still more skilled than the student. That is how it should be."

"You sound like Da," Elliun grumbled.

"Really? I think I like that."

Daven Talvi, the strongest mage in the Bitterroot clan, was certainly a great role model for any of them. The fact that Elliun compared Max to his grandfather certainly pleased him. *Maybe I am doing this right, after all.*

He sniffed the air, sensing a change in the wind, and then peered up through the heavy fir branches. "Come on, let's move along. I think rain's coming in."

Elliun made a face. "It better clear up before it's time for the ritual. Momma will be unhappy. And no one likes that."

Max bit his lip. He had seen Jelani's temper often enough to know what Elliun said was one hundred percent true. "Agreed." He checked once more for signs of danger, and then led the way out of the clearing and toward the valley. The day's lessons were far from over.

CHAPTER 11

JELANI could have waited for information from the scouts Astan was sure to send out, sizing up the threat level of this DeLuna woman. But she had always been a 'do it yourself' kind of girl. Discovery by the outer world would have far too many consequences to leave this to chance. She wanted to observe for herself. So one afternoon, while Kayli spent a few hours with Djana and the Circle, Jelani went to see what she could find.

She chose a jacket in the soft shades of green and sienna, over brown pants, and put on a pair of strong boots for there was still snow in the upper passes of the mountain. Jelani made her way along an obscure path in the forest, one even the elves did not use often, as she hiked the twenty miles to the place of the *Donoma.*

She felt guilty for leaving her daughter with the Circle. Years before, they had tried to force her to conceive a daughter to be the next queen of the clan. She had fooled them, thanks to her stubborn nature and the Butterfly Herbs coffee she loved. Somehow it had changed her chemistry and brought her a son instead. Once she dutifully produced the heir to the clan throne, all was well between her and the Circle. At least as far as it appeared. One thing she was sure of was that Djana and the others would never hurt Kayli. They would likely lay down their own lives before they would let anyone do so. For now, that was good enough for her.

The breeze that came down the mountain was cool and fresh, filled with the warmth of the sun and the scent of wildflowers. Above her head, that breeze whispered through the branches of the pine trees, stimulating birdsong that spurred her along the way. Some small waterfall, unseen among the rocks, rippled a sweet harmony to the birds' tune, almost like the tinkling of a well tuned piano. Her boots kept time like the best of the percussion section, rounding out the natural orchestra.

Old Sister Maria was right. The hills are alive with the sound of music, but without the flederhorn and the other crazy Alpine instruments. Who needs that when you have all this?

Her breaths came deep and clear as she walked quickly on her chosen path. Her old self, barista and college dropout Jelani Marsh, would have been begging to stop by now. She was lucky if she walked seven or eight blocks in a day. What a change! Since Jelani had come back to the woods after Elliun was found, and the clan put back in order again, she had returned to her role as caretaker of these forests, spending many hours a day tending and healing the harms that humans did, even unintentionally, to the clan lands.

She had asked Daven once if it would be possible to create a blanket protection, something that would keep humans from even entering upon their land.

"Did that work for your Native Americans?" Daven replied. "Their shamans certainly commanded powerful magic."

She frowned. "It's not the same."

"But it is. No one species or culture controls magic." He laughed softly. "Too many people in the world. What Lane does with those machines on his desk would seem the greatest magic they'd ever experienced. Who's to say it is not?"

Maybe he was right. Who was she kidding? Daven always ended up right, one way or another. But even if it could be done, a sudden change of such a nature would definitely be noticed, explored and investigated by the very people they wanted to keep away.

So instead, she used the powers of the *Donoma* to extend her natural gifts, setting wounded trees to grow again, sparking new life in old forests, promoting fertility among the animal herds and families of the area. The cycling of energy through these life forms improved the lives of the elves, along with the humans who shared their space. Creating new energies to be returned to the earth, ready to heal and sustain them again.

And I'm not about to risk all that for the sake of someone's crappy television show.

Jelani had not seen this show, but then it had been a couple of years since she had watched much television other than an occasional glimpse while she visited Lane and Crispy. She had never been a great fan before she moved up to the forest. Not much on the tube seemed more important than work or hanging out with friends. But she was familiar with the style of these expose type reporters.

All we have to do is make sure this chick ends up with the same result.

A small smile inched across her lips as she contemplated egg on the woman's face, and the thought spurred her steps, drawing her into an easy run. Her time with the elves had adjusted her body to an efficient machine. Elves ran most places outside their small enclave. She moved lightly now, like the others, hardly leaving a trace that she had passed, no matter how many miles she traveled.

When she crested a hill leading down to the feeder stream, she was hit with a wave of dizziness that knocked her from her feet as surely as if she had hit a wall. Head spinning, she struggled to her feet, grabbing the nearest tree trunk for support, letting its rough bark bruise her fingers to focus her attention anywhere but that nausea inducing whirlwind inside her.

The Donoma shouldn't be anywhere near here. What the hell is going on?

She tried to think, but could not fight the sensations shaking her. Escape was the only option. She dropped to her knees and then her elbows, rolling away down the hill toward the stream, doing her best to protect her face with her arms, still coming up scratched and out of breath when she hit the bottom.

But it was gone.

She looked up at the spot where she had stood, the wandering vortex invisible as before, waiting for its next unsuspecting victim. That was it, of course. 'Unsuspecting' was the key. When the elves channeled the energy with proper magic during rituals, and it was where it belonged, a nice, even transfer of the surge took place. This, though, was potentially dangerous.

A little better prepared, she brushed herself off, hoping she would not encounter more shattered bits of the original, twisting and turning in their own small orbits. Whatever the commercial vortex site used for its own purposes seemed fairly stable, even though it fed off from the main source of power deep in the earth. This, whatever it was, needed to be healed as soon as possible. With a little more urgency in her step, she hurried on.

Jelani encountered several sets of people hiking through the woods, and she purposely slowed to greet each group, English coming to her tongue as easily as the Elvish language she now spoke among her brothers and sisters of the clan. She wanted to get a read on them, looking for those who might mean trouble. All seemed to be proper tourists with varied gear, backpacks, hiking boots, water bottles strapped to their waists, simply out to enjoy the beautiful Bitterroots for a summer afternoon.

Perhaps Lane's concerns had been exaggerated by his innate paranoia.

Near the end of her intended journey, still two miles from the commercial entrance on Highway 2 to the vortex property, she heard voices and paused, detecting a decided shrillness in a woman's voice that did not sound like most of the tree huggers who admired and loved this wild area.

"This is impossible. How can I find something that's invisible?"

A man countered the woman, his voice calm in contrast. "It's more of a feeling, Chiara. The only 'marker' that you'll find is back there at the office. We've been through there twice, and you said you felt the earth move in that circle of trees."

The woman was defensive now. "I *did* feel the earth move. The world seemed to be tipped at a forty five degree angle, especially when I closed my eyes."

"That same feeling should come to you, even out here. It may be strongest on the property there, which is why the Haubers set up the original site to demonstrate it to people. The state took about thirty eight acres of it back in the 1980s by eminent domain, the part that heads back toward the river. No one's ever proved what effects it has back here."

Jelani's back crinkled with a sudden set of goose bumps as she realized this was the very woman she was looking for. Was she already filming? The man could be a member of her crew. She inched closer, choosing not to be seen, peering from behind a thick clump of trees.

The woman was medium height, with a chic blonde cut to her hair, wearing some sort of unattractive pale blue pantsuit that probably cost a fortune. She teetered on mid-heeled strappy sandals, apparently finding the forest floor a little lumpy with fallen sticks and outgrown roots. In her right hand was a small video camera, and as Jelani watched, the woman swung it slowly from side to side, taking in a panorama of the spot where she stood.

"The tour guide said he believed there was another location out here to the west that was nearly as strong as the aura spot place inside."

He shrugged. "Would have been more helpful if he had given you GPS coordinates."

Jelani turned her attention to the man, finding him a much more usual trespasser in the mountains, dressed in jeans, boots and a thick vest. He had no equipment. Must be some sort of guide. *What right does he have to bring her to our energy source?*

"It certainly would." The woman muttered and stumbled around in her shoes, tromping the low cover of new vegetation. Jelani studied the man, seeing his barely covered amusement at her predicament. So perhaps he was not fully committed to whatever insanity she intended to let loose here.

"Maybe if we—"

"Just give me a minute!" she snapped. She tucked the camera in her jacket pocket and closed her eyes. Holding both hands out in front of her like the actors in a bad zombie movie, she moved, first forward, and then off to the right. "This way."

The man sighed, but followed her. Jelani, too, skirted the trees to remain out of sight, but kept up with the investigator, her heart picking up a little extra speed because the crazy woman was headed straight for the river spot where the ritual would take place in less than three days.

How did she know?

What am I going to do?

The Circle had finally ceded its authority over to her, certainly in a grudging way at first, but in the last year or so, almost lovingly. *Except for Djana, but she would never forgive me for not choosing Daven as mate.* They relied on her to keep the clan safe. How would she frighten this woman away in a manner that would not just intrigue her more?

Suddenly several large crows, complaining in their angry, raucous tone, flew into the clearing, coming directly for the woman. The wing flapping, squawking and extended claws made the big black birds seem even larger and more dangerous than Jelani knew them to be. She ducked down behind a tree trunk, torn between the opportunity to rescue the woman and suggest she get the hell out of Dodge, and the delight at watching the deterrence happen without her involvement.

Chiara screamed and covered her head with her arms as the birds dived close to her. The man with her ran over to shoo the birds, but they did not let up, even when he waved his walking stick in a way that nearly hit them. Jelani was surprised. The crows seemed very determined, for crows. They did not generally exhibit the kind of personality to really pursue such an attack. After several chaotic minutes, Jelani began to wonder what their motive might be. The TV host was not wearing anything sparkly, a mistake that might have attracted the crows in the first place.

A sound up in a tree to her left caught her attention. She glanced up. Movement in the branches above her head might not feel like more than the wind to outsiders, but she recognized the soft steps of her kind.

She inched backward, staying out of sight of the couple fighting off the birds, and finally caught a glimpse of Elron, one arm hooked around the tree trunk for stability, and the other waving the birds on, a huge smile on his face. He looked over his shoulder beyond him to another tree where Beckley's thick body clung to another tree, much less stable but no less determined, by the look on his face.

Elron did not let up, nor did it take the couple long before they hurried off toward their parked sport utility vehicle. The woman continued to let out panicked yelps, though Jelani did not notice any blood. She had to give Elron extra points for control. The wheel of the vehicle spun hard, sending wood and rocks flying as it took off in the direction of the main road.

The crows flew away, still cawing, and Jelani sat back on a broken tree trunk, wondering whether the woman did have the power to track their source. If she did have the power, what then? This year the clan's ritual was not just a matter of tradition. Though the summer solstice was the longest day, and the energy connected with the mages at that time in a way it could on no other, what she had experienced up the hill must be taken into consideration. The *Donoma* was out of control.

At the very least, they must have the ritual as scheduled, and it must be at the location where they best accessed the swirling energies as they came to the surface of the earth. Three days. That was all they needed.

Maybe they had put the woman off enough with this little stunt that she would go back to her cushy hotel and have fainting fits for a few days, and not return until the ritual had passed. Once they had reconnected the vortex arms, turning it into a calm, strong stream once again, these outbreaks that had gotten the attention of the outside world would fade into a more dormant state. The television woman could hunt for it all over then, and she would not find a thing.

Three days. Was it so much to ask?

CHAPTER 12

LANE paused in his tapping of keyboards, the silence from the other room gnawing at his nerves. "Crisp, have you talked to Iris yet?"

Crispy's answer was muffled behind the bathroom door.

"What?"

Nothing.

Lane's foot tapped a staccato tango. Crispy had not been out of the apartment in two weeks, and had not been farther than the corner in much longer. Lane had been afraid to push him too hard, worried he would retreat even farther into his own world, back as he had been when they had originally moved in together. No one wanted that.

After Jelani first moved to clan territory, Crispy was a constant visitor, especially after the birth of Elliun. Lane thought the two had a special bond after Jelani and Astan stayed with them while running from Bartolomey. Despite all that, the visits became less frequent until they stopped altogether. The new baby was only six months old and Crispy had hardly seen the sprout in her own home.

This was ridiculous, and apparently Daven Talvi's fault.

"Why do our troubles always seem to begin and end with the elves?" Lane muttered. He fidgeted in his chair a few more moments. When the bathroom door opened, he jumped up and made a beeline for the bedroom before Crispy could close the door.

"Hey—" Crispy protested weakly, but Lane was determined this time.

"Look, man. I know you don't want to talk about this, but I think we have to." Lane stood in the doorway, blocking it from being closed with his hefty body. "You've been hiding in this apartment for weeks now and you need to talk to someone about it. If not Iris, then someone else. You've got a good life outside these walls, and I want to know why you're neglecting it."

Crispy turned away. "I can stay here if I want." His tone implied the corollary 'you're not the boss of me'.

"Sure you can. But why would you want to?" Lane leaned his left shoulder against the wall. "Especially now that Jelly Bean needs us."

Crispy chewed his bottom lip. "She needs *you*. I'm not good for...."

Lane's temper flared as his roommate started into the old cycle, and it must have showed in his eyes, because Crispy broke off in mid-sentence.

"She needs us. Both of us. That crazy TV woman is on their trail and she's going to cause all sorts of havoc if we don't stop her."

Crispy stared at the floor, nodding at last without a verbal response.

Annoyed at the fates that had made him his brother's keeper, Lane cleared his throat, knowing he was about to tread into dangerous territory. "Crisp, is this about Sammy?"

A visible tremor ran through Crispy, but he shook his head.

Well, maybe he really moved past that, then. Lane took a deep breath, blew it out slowly, mentally casting about for a direction to proceed. "I want to help you, but if you don't let this out, I honestly just don't know how."

Thinking it might be less threatening if he moved out of the doorway, Lane took the chance Crispy would bolt and walked over to take a seat on his own bed. Crispy then retreated into his beanbag chair, pulling his worn quilted blanket over him, even though it was mid-afternoon and ninety degrees outside.

"So what is bugging you?"

Crispy picked at the blanket's edge, pulling at a loose thread.

Lane tried to relax and be patient, but this stonewalling made him crazy. How did Iris do this job all day every day? He had no clue.

"Look, bro, we've been through everything together, right? You know all my dark, dirty secrets, all the things my uncle did to me when I was a kid, how my mother used to shoot up the house. I know about your mom and all the other things we went through at the foster home. Nothing you say is going to shock me at this point." He wondered whether levity would help' and decided it might. "Unless you tell me you've bought a pink ballerina tutu to wear, or something."

That drew a sharp, startled look.

At least I've got his attention.

Or else he's bought a pink ballerina tutu to wear. Holy mother of Baryshnikov battles!

"Maybe I don't need to know that. But we're all worried about you. And like I said, we need you. This ritual's coming up really fast, and Daven said you should be there for it."

Crispy sighed and kept picking at the blanket.

"Remember last year when we went? We all felt better for days. Your hawk even flew over."

Now that was stretching it, Lane admitted silently. Crispy insisted he had seen the hawk he and Astan had healed years before, and not for the first time. After it had helped protect Elliun after the attack on the queen, he often commented how he had encountered it in the forest doing this or that. But could it still have been the same one? Lane had no idea. He did not think so.

How long did hawks live, anyway? Why was he even thinking about this?

Delicious, stress reducing cupcakes called to him from the kitchen. *Not now.* He dragged his mind back to the subject at hand. If Crispy would not tell him what was going on, then Lane was going to haul Iris here to deal with it.

He studied Crispy's somber expression, wishing he had some of his online persona's gifts, and he could just read his roommate's mind. *Wouldn't that save a lot of time?* "I could just start guessing. How's this? You wave at me when I get to the right subject, okay?"

Crispy did not answer.

With a sinking feeling in his stomach, Lane plunged in. "You already said it wasn't Sammy. Have you been thinking about your mom? The old neighborhood? Are you worried about the pollutions in the valley? Expecting aliens to show up and abduct you? I know you can't be worried about Black Bart and his people because they're gone."

Crispy stiffened up, his fingers clenched on the hem of the blanket.

"That's it? Bart and his people? Why would they still be around?" Lane frowned, puzzled. "We beat them, remember? He's gone, and his people, most of them are repatriated into the clan. Even that Vez dude, like he's brainwashed back into a fuzzy teddy bear now."

Crispy shook his head.

"Not Bart or Vez. Really, Crisp, the war's over. Everyone's happy again."

"Not…the war."

Not the war? What did that mean?

Granted, Crispy had been on the outside of that series of events. Lane had been the one dead center, even being drafted as a mage of the clan as a representative of the human world. So if not that, then what?

"None of those guys are still around, Crisp. The ones that wouldn't come back to the fold all faded away, even the ones from the first round. Really."

Even as he said it, though, the answer hit him. It was the ones from the first round. That awful scene when Lane, Astan, Iris and Crispy thought Daven was dead and Jelani could be, too, and that cobra man elf had hypnotized them all. All except Crispy.

But that was long ago.

The voices of multiple therapists over the years filtered through Lane's mind, reminding him that post traumatic stress could manifest immediately or many years later, depending on the person. And since Daven buried so much of that for Crispy, thinking he was being kind at the time, how likely was it that the damage might only now surfacing?

Treading carefully, Lane modulated his voice into a gentler mode. "You saved everyone, you know. None of us anticipated that guy. You were the only one who was able to take action." Lane shifted uncomfortably. "I'd have shot him if he hadn't gotten me first. You did the right thing."

His face a mask of misery, Crispy pulled the blanket up over his head.

Feeling better now that he had at least discovered the right subject, Lane sighed. "Do you want me to call Iris? Even if she's not your official therapist, I bet she'd help you with this."

After he had spoken, Lane realized that it would have to be Iris. How could Crispy share this story with anyone else? Elves? Magic? Blue Screen of Death? Any regular therapist would have him locked up for a break with reality.

The lumpy blanket pile that was Crispy moved a little and then he emerged, looking defeated. "All right."

"All right then. I'll call her. But you've got to come to the ritual, even if she can't see you before then, please? Daven asked specifically that I bring you along. I think he's got something in mind that might help. Okay?"

A shrug came in response.

That was probably all he was likely to get on that topic. He remained reluctant to push too hard. "So what about this investigator? Got any ideas how to scare her off?"

He smiled faintly. "Aliens?"

"Do you have some?" Lane let himself relax a little. "Although…maybe that would be just the thing she wants to see."

* * *

CHIARA fumed all the way back to the hotel. "Crows attacking? Really? Just when we were about to track down this energy source? Do you think that was a coincidence?"

Curran's face set in determined lines as he drove back to the highway. "I don't know what could have set them off."

She eyed him sidewise. Did something critical underline his

words? Did he think she was nuts? "I certainly didn't see anything."

He shook his head. "I didn't either. In all my years in the Bitterroot, I haven't seen anything quite like that." His eyes flicked left and then right, before he turned onto the main road. "Maybe there was a nest nearby. We could have disturbed a mating pair."

Am I reading too much into this?

She did not like questioning her perceptions, because she usually just *knew* things. Something else had been at work out there, and she did not believe it was a mating pair or a nest or anything that straightforward. The forces of the earth had acted on her body, leading her in the direction she had been going, ever since she walked the labyrinth in the middle of the vortex site. Something was out there.

And you're running away. The thought slapped her, bringing a hot flush to her cheeks.

What would Hunter say? Tears stung her eyes, and she turned away to look out the passenger window.

"Do you want to go back?"

Curran's question was offered in a gentle, solicitous tone that Chiara took for pity. That hardened her response. "No. I've got to meet with the camera crew. They're due in this morning."

"Do we need to pick them up?"

"No. They've brought their equipment, so they'll just put it in their rental vehicle."

"You're ready to film?" He sounded surprised.

She tried not to growl at him. "I've got the commercial Vortex site ready to go. Some of it may be corny, but I'm willing to bet that the crew has some odd experiences out there, just like we did."

"I still don't see how that ladder trick works. How can you be heavier on one side of it than the other?"

"Maybe it's not a trick," she said, her mind already distracted by the thought of setting up camera angles and spots to do on camera interviews. *One right in front of that Golden Door. Definitely a sequence in the Mystery House.*

"The people at the Vortex office sure seemed real open about people testing out all these things and taking pictures," Curran said.

"They did, didn't they?"

Chiara had been fascinated by the fast talking tour guide, who demonstrated the 'amazing' transformation of the people who honestly appeared taller or shorter depending on where they stood on a marked circle on various pieces of ground. The guide claimed it was because of the vortex energy. Chiara had not made up her mind about that yet. Once the crew came, it would be easy to determine. They would have suitcases full of ELF Teslameters, RF detectors, geomagnetometers, pocket field meters, and much more. These things could document in hard numbers what heightened senses told her. Something extraordinary, perhaps even magical, was going on here.

Even if they did not, she would still believe. She felt the tug, the pull, the twisting sensation in the aura spot. She had seen her own aura, a faint brown smoky color surrounding her hand, stretching down to her feet. What did a brown aura mean? It was the color of earth, right? That should be something strong. Perhaps it meant she was getting closer to the mystery.

But she did not think so. If it was anything like a mood ring, she was definitely in trouble.

No. I refuse to accept that.

This show was not in trouble, just sidetracked by a couple of bad days. She could be professional. Get her job done right and then everything in her world would fall back into place again. She would either make or break right here.

"Chiara?"

She glanced at Curran, who watched her with a concerned face. "Hmm?"

"Are you all right? You seem to be miles away."

Miles away, all right. Back at my desk in New York, where people are calling me for help and publicity, not the other way around. "Sorry. Just thinking about the shoot."

He smiled. "Thanks for including me in this. It's very exciting."

His genuine pleasure rebuked her for escaping into her own world. Curran really was providing her with much needed support and services. The least she could do would be to pay attention.

"You're welcome. I couldn't be getting so much done without your help. You know what? I bet we'll need a guinea pig for some of the demonstrations in our clips. That should be you. Are you up to it?"

The delighted spark that entered his eyes left no question of his response. "I think I can manage that."

"Great. We'll get started as soon as we get back."

Her driver happy, her plans underway, Chiara settled into the seat and let her thoughts drift back to how she would make Hunter beg to be her lover once again. After what he had put her through, she would not make it easy.

CHAPTER 13

"ELLIUN?"

Max glanced around the small, pine filled glade, suddenly aware that the prince was gone. Again. Panic flashed through his heart like an arrow. With his family engaged in preparations for the *Donoma* ritual, the prince had been left in Max's care a great deal over the last several days, and he was beginning to rebel.

"No one else has to learn the names of all the plants in the forest," Elliun complained. "And practice magic for two hours at a time!"

That was the first argument that morning. Fortunately, it was not until they were out of earshot of the tree house, so Max was not humiliated right out of the gate. No amount of explaining seemed to satisfy him. Elliun could not understand that because his mother was queen, he needed to know more than others did. The prince seemed all too happy to receive special privileges, but he did not want to engage in any of the responsibilities or burdens that came with the same lineage.

Of course not. He's hardly old enough to even be considered a Younger yet. They do expect so much from him. But it's not up to me to deviate from their plan.

So Max spent the rest of the morning trying to find new, interesting things to do, to keep his student engaged. He pulled out a dozen magical skills he had been taught over his lifetime, but Elliun did not focus well enough to grasp any of them. He became frustrated and quit.

Max needed a break, so he set Elliun free to burn off some of that wild energy, and directed him to return when he heard Max's call. But he did not come back.

Frantic, he searched the woods around the last place he had seen the prince. Not even a footprint to lead him in the right direction. Max climbed the nearest tree, half airborne in his fierce panic. From twenty five feet above the ground, he could see for some distance, and he circled the tree, moving gingerly from branch to branch, using his natural lightness to flit lightly while his eyes scanned the ground below.

There.

Elliun was heading away from the clan lands, toward the western mountains, at a run. A hundred different horrible scenarios went through his mind. *I've got to get there right now.*

Without a second thought, he launched himself right from the tree branch, willing himself to glide at the shallowest angle possible down to the ground, but his tight nerves threw off his aim and he crashed into the lower branches of a spruce tree, its needles raking his skin. Startled, he fell to the ground, rolling down the small hill at the foot of the tree. A shocked moment passed while he caught his breath. When he could breathe again, he scrambled to his feet and started to run. He came around a small stand of trees and nearly smacked right into the prince with his grandfather.

"And here's Max now," said Daven Talvi, a warm smile on his face, one arm around Elliun's shoulders.

Breathing as if he had just run a race, Max fought to remain upright as his head filled with a misty dizziness. One look at Elliun's face, though, showed that Max was not the only one distressed.

Daven hesitated and cocked his head. "We should move from this place," he said, his voice soft but no less a command. He slipped his other arm around Max's shoulders and physically moved the two with him several elf lengths to the south, before turning back to look at the spot where they had been. *It's coming.*

Max heard his thought even though it was not spoken aloud. The worry in Daven's mental tone alarmed him. What was coming? When?

He did not have to wait long. The ground shook all around them, causing Elliun to grab onto his grandfather's leg. Then the world seemed to skew sideways, and Max fought to keep his feet.

The small saplings in the place where they had been standing swayed and bent as if a mountain wind blasted them, but he could detect no motion in the air at all. The phenomenon went on for several long seconds, perhaps a hundred heartbeats, and then the shaking stopped.

Max found he could stand upright again, not pressed by the invisible forces. But the young trees remained in their tortured, bent configuration, as though a spiraling tornado had burst up through the ground and left them in that shape to commemorate its passing.

"The *Donoma*?" Max asked, staring in wonder.

Daven nodded. "And miles from where it should be." He sighed.

Elliun inched closer to the distorted copse, his usual bravado missing in action. Receiving no ill effect from touching the branches, he cautiously explored the small area, finding it fascinating.

Soon Daven beckoned him to join them again. "Perhaps this would be the time to apologize to Max for running off and upsetting him."

Elliun's jaw set and his lip popped out in a pout. "But, Da...."

Daven's hand patted Elliun's shoulder. "Max carries a great responsibility every day as your teacher, instructing you about the ways of our clan. He did not have to take on this chore. He volunteered. His is a most important part in the interwoven web of our daily lives. If we did not have confidence in his ability to show you all you must know, then you would not be relegated to his care."

Max felt a small chill of unease. What was Daven saying? That Max was not living up to the level expected of him? He straightened his shoulders, trying to stand a little taller. He could do this. He could. If Elliun would just cooperate and let Max teach him.

Daven waited, patient as the river wearing away at a rock face, his eyes locked with those of the stubborn elf child.

Finally, Elliun turned to Max. "I'm sorry," he said. "I

shouldn't make you worry."

Daven's glance at Max was loaded.

It's a test, then. Max struggled a moment with what to say. He crouched down until he was eye level with the child. "I want you to be the best elf you can be," he said. "I'm glad you're willing to work with me to do that."

Elliun's frustrated expression was so much like his mother's, Max was taken aback. No one wanted to be on the bad side of the queen when she looked that way.

Daven chuckled. "Now, go find me some healing herbs, Elliun. There's a patch of the tall stems with the yellow flowers just down by the stream to the right. There, and no farther."

Elliun lost no time in escaping their intent regard and scooted away into the bush.

Max could not help a sigh, drawing Daven's attention.

"You have no reason to be disappointed," Daven said. "You're doing as well as anyone could."

Unconvinced, Max plopped down on the worn trunk of a fallen tree. "You don't need to say that just to cheer me up."

Daven sat next to him, a reassuring, strong presence. "Why would I do that? Elliun's safety and upbringing is as important to me as my own life. I wouldn't waste my breath on meaningless words."

Feeling a little star struck that the clan's mage sat with him, just like any other ordinary *nian*, Max fidgeted, thinking of something to say that did not sound idiotic. "I try so hard with him. I want him to have the same experiences as we all did, growing up. He's too anxious to be an adult. He needs to be a child."

Daven smiled. "That's very perceptive of you. Astan and I have discussed this on many occasions. In a normal elf home, he would have much more opportunity to do that, but Astan and Jelani have such diverse responsibilities that they don't always have time to…." Daven's lips pressed together a moment. "Can I be candid with you?"

Max sat up a little straighter, surprised and honored that

Daven would take him into his confidence. "Of course."

Daven took a deep breath and leaned back a little, staring off at the horizon. "Jelani's return to the Bitterroot clan has been for the best, and I think everyone agrees on this. We've put the divisions in the clan behind us, and we've been able to heal the worst wounds. But for all those successes, there is no question that in coming from the human world Jelani has brought new and different ways to the clan. She has to spend a lot of time entwining her intentions with those of the Circle and the rest of us. The traditions weigh her down and she fights against them. She rebels."

Daven gestured toward Elliun. "He is many things, but most of all he is his mother's child. Even his conception went awry. He should have been born a female, the next queen of the clan. Instead, he is the charming young lad you have volunteered to take on."

"Mmm-hmm." Max felt a smile tug at his lips.

"By working against such a rough object, you too, will benefit. He will challenge you, he will bring you to the brink of losing your mind, but most of all he will sharpen and polish you. In the long run, teaching Elliun will not only bring him to a fine understanding of all he must know, but it will also demonstrate to others in the clan what a fine young *nian* you are as well."

Max shot Daven a sidewise look, half wondering if he was being manipulate, but the mage seemed quite sincere.

Daven grinned. "Who better to look after and teach one who is unlike all the others than another unique individual?" He reached for Max's shoulder and gave it a warm squeeze. "You belong together. You'll get through this, and he'll be thankful in the long run. You'll see."

The mage's touch was reassuring and made Max feel confident and capable. *So this is what The Lane means by 'whammied'. I think I like it.*

"Thank you, Daven. I appreciate your kind words."

"I'm pleased to share them with you, Max. Sometimes I think none of us complement each other as often as we should. You should know that if the queen did not trust you with her son, you would not be his companion. I trust her choice."

The place where Daven's hand touched him warmed and even throbbed a little, but not in a painful way. The feeling punctuated Daven's words, made them seem like a foregone conclusion, something that Max should never have questioned. He stood up, his head full of light, a little wobbly with goodwill, prepared now to begin the afternoon.

"What lessons do you have yet to conquer today?" Daven asked.

"Perhaps I shall teach Elliun to fly," Max said, half teasing.

Daven's concerned expression made Max laugh.

"No, don't worry. I won't do that. Not yet. He is dangerous enough on the ground. I'll keep a closer grip on him the rest of the day, though. Too many bad things can happen if he gets out of reach."

"Agreed. If you find yourself in need of help, let me know. I'm sure I can come up with some new ideas for the both of you."

Elliun appeared at the edge of the glade with two handfuls of herbs. He eyed Max and then Daven, as if deciding whether they were now some sort of co-conspirators. "I have your weeds," he said to Daven.

"So you do." The mage walked over to his grandson and collected the bruised stems, taking a moment to inhale their scent.

"What is that stuff?" Elliun said. "It stinks."

"The humans call it monkey flower. When we steam the crushed leaves, it will relieve sore muscles for those of us aging faster than we'd like to admit."

Elliun ignored Daven's self deprecating grin and threw his arms around Daven's legs. "You're not getting old, Da. You'll be with us forever."

"Whoa, there. Don't worry your head about me." Daven held the herbs in one hand and patted the child with the other. "We'll have many more days in the sun and snow. But I've got to take these back to the clan lands for Pieter and you have Max to attend to. Go on, now."

He patted the boy on the head and nodded a farewell to Max. Then he walked away into the woods, where Max would swear he simply vanished. After a deep breath, Max got back to business.

"Time to explore the bear's cave," Max announced. "Are you ready?"

CHAPTER 14

ONCE her team arrived, Chiara felt like her life was back on its proper track.

She booked three more rooms on the same floor as her own, one for the two cameramen, one for the equipment carrier. Janie had also flown out to be script girl, gopher, and occasional whipping girl. They had arrived just as it was it was getting dark the night before. This morning, she found her crew standing outside ogling the natural beauty.

"Haven't you people ever been outdoors?" she finally asked, having chased them down in the far end of the parking lot, finding them pointing at the snow atop the nearest mountains.

"Have you smelled this air?" Janie asked.

Chiara let out an exasperated sigh. "Yes, Janie. It's air. Just like air anywhere."

"Oh no, boss lady," Artie the cameraman said. He rubbed his scruffy, beard covered chin and reached up to the sky. "This is air. It smells like…grass. Like something alive."

The equipment guy, Steve, nodded vehemently. "In case you don't remember, New York smells like a big bag of decaying, moldy garbage buried in a men's locker room."

Chiara inhaled deeply, finding no reason to disagree. Montana air was filled with an aroma she had not smelled since she was a child. It was fresh, sweet, with just a hint of chilly mountain mist in the early mornings, the scent of wildflowers at the height of the day and the wide open sky packed with stars at night. She could definitely understand their amazement, for she shared it.

"I know guys. But we're on budget. *And* deadline. We've got to get this nailed in three days. Right?"

"Yeah," Steve said, his voice dripping with reluctance.

"Come on, let's load up!" Janie stole a last, long look at the stellar vista around them, and then smacked her clipboard with her right hand. "Chop, chop."

Muttering complaints, they scrambled inside, grabbing the equipment they had carried down to the lobby earlier and loading it into the silver sports utility vehicle they rented for the occasion. Since the crew had no personality conflicts with the airlines, they had flown into the small airport just south of Glacier, so their trip to the resort had been much shorter. Chiara tried not to be jealous.

Besides, I got the opportunity to meet Curran, right?

Janie drove and Chiara made notes on the way out to the Vortex site, talking over her shoulder to the men, unable to stop herself from micromanaging the shoot. She went over the shots she wanted so many times that Artie finally cut her off.

"Yeah, we got it, boss lady. We read the memo. At least once."

"You've got the multi field meter? And the electro sensor? In case the presences show up that the guide was talking about. The lights in the pictures, the otherworldly lights?"

Artie's eyes narrowed.

"All right, all right." She fidgeted in the passenger seat. "You know there's a lot riding on this, that's all."

A long silence fell as Janie weaved through semi-trucks carrying huge piles of giant logs along highway two as they came into downtown Columbia Falls, a town with some seriously beautiful Victorian homes and a whole strip of tourist oriented shops heavily featuring huckleberries. Chiara did not even know what a huckleberry was. She had thought it was some kind of dog at first, but that did not seem to go with any of the brightly painted signs. The guys in the crew, though, were already demanding a midmorning break to try some huckleberry pie.

"Maybe when we get this wrapped," Chiara said, in a voice that meant 'no'.

After that, more silence.

"He hasn't called?" Janie finally asked.

Chiara shot her a look. She did not intend to discuss her love life in front of the crew. Stealing a glance over her shoulder, she saw all the guys looking away uncomfortably. *Oh, hell. Not like they don't know it already. It doesn't matter. I'm not giving them the satisfaction of seeing the damned cracks in my armor.*

"I've been so busy I haven't checked messages very much," she said.

"Oh." Her tone one of disbelief, Janie's jaw set in her usual stubborn oppositional mode. "How far up is this place?"

"Right there!" Chiara pointed frantically as Janie squealed the brakes, yanking the wheel to put the vehicle into the turn lane.

They pulled into the large front parking lot, with its oversized carved wooden animals out front, the cabin like store that led into the back area where the energy spikes would be found.

"The House of Mystery?" Steve snickered from the backseat. "Bet the only mysterious thing is why people plunk down money to get in here. How much was it again?"

Chiara felt determination and defensiveness stiffen her spine. "What do you care? You're not paying it. Let's see what you say after you've been through the site."

She closed her eyes a moment, praying they would not mock the tour guide, who truly had a sideshow hawker delivery style, a little corny, but she had not really been interested in the guided tour. She appreciated the time after the tour, when those who had come to visit the site were left on their own to test the 'wonders' of the vortex property. That was when she was able to wander the area, feel the ragged bark of the twisted trees, sense the energy lines coming up through the ground and connect with the essence of the place. 'Something' real was there.

Her crew was there to take the instruments of science to the evidence of psychic or paranormal phenomena, and prove it or disprove it. Either way, it made a great story. She needed clips enough for an hour program, which meant three hours of filming or more, and she would be back on top of the investigation game.

She had certainly felt the power of the place when she visited with Curran. *I hope it's real. Opening up this area to those looking for a real psychic energy experience will put my name on everyone's lists.*

They bailed out of the vehicle, everyone picking up a case of equipment. Chiara grabbed the geomagnetometer, knowing just where she wanted to use it to detect the magnetic fields on the site. She hoped the guide would retreat to the shop, like he did the first time. She intended to sneak out back into the woods and use some of what the team had brought from New York to track down that pesky vortex flare she knew was there. She would have found it, if it had not been for those stupid crows.

The entrance was a gift shop, obviously designed for tourists. She heard a groan behind her from one of the guys, but she plunged on. She stopped at the counter, laying down her credit card to pay their entrance fees.

"Back again, Miss DeLuna?" The proprietor glanced up at her with twinkling blue eyes, not the suspicious drawing back she usually experienced once her crew appeared on the scene. "Good. We like it when people come to test us out."

A *sotto voce* comment from her camera guy drew a swift kick in the shin. Chiara pasted a bright smile to her lips. "We're fascinated by what you have to offer here."

The guy clearly knew who she was. "We've been trying to get someone of your stature to visit for the longest time. I know you'll do us proud."

She kept that smile locked tight. "It's a mysterious site that we certainly want to share with the world."

He beamed. "Great. I know you took the tour the other day with your friend. You probably know as much about what we do here as our guide. Fred's not in yet this morning. Something about a flat tire, his wife said when she called. But I trust you. Why don't you take your team out into the woods?"

Startled at the change in routine, she skipped herself into recovery. "Of course. Thank you."

Grabbing her geomagnetometer, she headed for the door at the rear of the gift shop, her team taking a moment to realize they had been dismissed. They scrambled after her, dragging their equipment. It was not until they got out to the first turn of the little wood fenced path that Janie ventured a question.

"Friend?"

Chiara stiffened. She had not mentioned Curran to the crew. In fact, she did not intend on saying anything about him, but there it was. The image of his face popped into her mind, that half smile and the dreamy expression he had shared just the day before as they stood in the shallows of Yaak River. Curran seemed so nice, so kind, something her ego desperately needed right now. But he was not Hunter Nowles.

And the last thing she needed was a whiff of this getting back to Hunter. Or was it?

She quickly calculated the value of sparking a little jealousy in her ambitious ex-lover. Perhaps he only glommed on to her with the hope of riding her coattails to paranormal investigation glory. He deserves it if someone else stepped into that spot.

"Didn't I mention him? Curran Tanner. Local expert on the Bitterroot Mountains and the forest systems. He's been extremely helpful the last several days, showing me around the area. He seems to know just everyone." She turned to face them, thinking of Curran's smile again, and felt a warm glow creep up under her cheeks.

Janie's eyes widened. "Oh, my land. You've been seeing him. Like, 'seeing him'."

Perfect. "Janie, honey, you know I only *see* ghosts and specters. Now come on. Let's get this done."

Staring off in any forward direction brought a view of trees as far as one could see. Huge stretches of it had likely not changed in seventy five years or more. If Chiara just stood and listened, she could swear she heard the rustle of someone going through the brush, echoes of the Native American Kootenai tribes that had passed in earlier times. Artie and Steve were both from the Midwest, so surely they had seen such a landscape. Janie, however, had grown up in good old New York City. She was obviously flabbergasted.

"It smells so good. And look how tall that tree is." Janie stopped and leaned her head back, peering all the way up the trunk until it seemed to vanish into the sky. "It must be a hundred years old."

Chiara laughed. "Probably more than that. But these aren't the fascinating ones. Come on."

She led the way around the little maze of fenced in path, pointing out the several trees that stood oddly tilted, loosely curved like a spiral noodle. "These are twisted by the energies coming from the earth," she said. "The vortex has done this to these trees."

Artie dutifully stopped to set up his camera, taking footage of the distorted trees that stood out from the rest by reaching tall and straight to the heavens. Chiara waited until that was done, and then hurried her chicks along to the trek uphill to the Mystery House.

In front of the House was a spot where the guide had showed them that, despite it being flat, as he had proved with a level he kept there just for that purpose, people who stood on one end would shrink and people who stood on the other end would become taller. It did not look like much, just a circle of concrete. And it certainly did not appear uneven. A mystery, indeed.

The theory was, as in several different places through the park, that the energies coming up through the earth altered perceptions and matter at the surface, making things appear in some way they were not. Chiara had not yet decided if she believed the theory. But she wanted to.

"Who's got a level?" she asked.

While Artie set up camera, Steve set down his backpack and dug in it, pulling out a yellow level about a foot long. He knelt down at the edge of the circle and set the instrument in the very center. They all observed as he leaned down to look at the result, Artie filming every breath holding second.

"It's flat here," Steve pronounced.

Chiara's excitement grew. "Try along all the edges. Especially the ones closest and farthest from the street."

The day she and Curran came here Chiara had been invited to be a test subject, but she declined, wanting instead to watch the process and test the results. She saw a little girl on the left side of the stone stand chest height to her father on the right, but when they changed places she almost reached his nose.

Chiara suspected that the tour guide's level had been altered in some way, and that the ground was not as level as it appeared. On the other hand, she was certainly willing to believe that some natural and mysterious force was at work. After all she had seen throughout her years of investigating, it would not surprise or shock her.

Steve dutifully measured, finding no discrepancies. "Seems flat as a board to me, boss."

Chiara nodded. "Wonderful." She ordered them into different poses there on the flat circle, in the same way the guide had the day before, petite Janie opposite slouching Steve, who was still a good six inches taller than her. At least on the right side of the circle. Chiara could see a definite diminution of that difference as they switched places.

I sure hope the camera gets all that.

She glanced over toward the building called House of Mystery and swallowed hard. "Now hold on to your stomachs."

The House of Mystery was said to be deeply possessed by the magic vortex energy. Their guide, Fred, had explained that the laws of gravity did not work in there. All Chiara knew was that entering the shadowy log building turned her stomach into knots. She could not even look across the room. Instead she focused on the floor or the ceiling as she pulled herself along the handrail to the center of the room, inching around the end of the rail to the clear space behind it. Then she found something safe to look at without getting sick.

She could not say exactly what did this to her. The guide explained it was the energies coming up through the earth in a most powerful way on this particular site, skewing the atmosphere. The floor was in fact tilted, and the interior of the house appeared to be upside down, so any disorientation would be natural, based on that alone.

Artie, camera on his shoulder, clung to the handrail, half hanging off it to get his footage. Chiara frowned, seeing how jerky the end of the camera was as it swung around. "Hold that steady, Art, or we won't have any picture to work with at all."

"I'm trying!" He adjusted his elbow around the rail and tried to shoot it again.

"Come toward the top side of the rail," she stated.

Artie inched his way up and around, mumbling under his breath.

Janie, meanwhile, seemed blissfully unaffected, and rushed all though the fifteen foot square building like a spring colt, checking out the items and features, including the ladder hanging from the ceiling. "What's this?" she asked.

Chiara forced her eyes to focus on the ladder, the pressures on her body making it a real effort. "They say if you try to crawl up the north side, the energies are working against you, but if you crawl up the south side, they're working for you. It's the same ladder, and you're climbing inches apart, but it's supposed to be a whole different experience."

"Really?" Janie's inquisitive face lit up and she immediately grabbed a rung. "Which side's north?"

Chiara had to orient herself a moment to make sure she was right. "It should be on the side away from me."

"Tell me when, Artie."

Artie had struggled to get his camera set up in a flat place for filming, but he finally got it together. "Go on."

Janie swung around to the north side, reaching up to a rung above her head, and she pulled herself up with a strained grunt. "Man, it's like I'm on one of the giant gas planets. I must weigh three hundred pounds." She gamely went up and down several times, the muscles standing out on her arms as she forced her transits. The last time she just jumped down, breathing hard.

"Now the other side," Chiara prompted.

Janie stepped around to the other side of the ladder, facing away from them. In just a moment, she shinnied all the way to the top. "Wow, that's like nothing." She did it several times more, her step light and airy.

"That's a crock," Steve said. "You come hold the boom."

So Janie and Steve changed places, and the same phenomenon occurred. Artie dropped a few disbelieving curse words, but kept filming. Chiara just tried not to get sick. *I hate this place.*

She imagined that it affected her because she was so sensitive. The swirling energies, though invisible, plowed through her body making her feel nauseous and heavy. Dwelling on it only made it worse. She wanted to escape the dark hole as quickly as possible.

"Artie, let's do a quick shot with me. Then I'll let you kids play, hmm?"

"Sure." Artie looked a little green, too. Not a good sign.

Chiara moved toward the ladder, only letting go of the handrail at the last second before the camera cranked on. She delivered a rehearsed speech about the nature of the vortex and how it might affect these things. Feeling a little like a hostess on a game show, she gestured in sequence to the different parts of the building that demonstrated the oddities and then gasped a final "Cut!" before heading for the far door.

Once on solid ground she waited for her head to stop spinning and the knot in her stomach to unclench. A pretty brass sculpture of a long legged bird sat in a tiny garden just outside the Mystery House, and she let the sunlight reflecting off its burnished body catch her attention, calm her and soothe her into a less volatile state.

"Is that it?" Artie called from the doorway. "What about these brooms?"

Ah, the brooms. No, they were not done at all. Chiara took a deep breath and went back to the doorway, keeping most of her focus on the outside instead of in that awful dimness. "They stand up by themselves."

"What?" Steve said. "Get out of here."

Chiara nodded. She not only had seen the phenomenon, she had been able to make it happen when she was here the other day. "The energies hold them up."

Janie eyed the diagonal cut bristles on the bottom of the brooms. "Bet that has something to do with it."

"It might." Chiara shrugged. "Try it."

As the camera kept a close watch, Janie took the broom and stood it straight, and then let it go. It crashed to the ground.

"Huh. Maybe you're not doing it right." Steve handed off the boom to Chiara and moved into camera range, taking the fallen broom. He tried it in several positions, but the only one that seemed to work was when the angle cut of the bristles aligned with the angle of the floor. Even so, it was not natural for a broom to remain upright without anyone holding it. 'Something' had to be at work here.

Once the filming was well under way, Chiara seized the opportunity to remain outside and move away from the nausea inducing house. While the Mystery House might be the showiest piece of the vortex site, it was certainly not the only one, and not the one that Chiara favored most. She had the labyrinth right in front of her, and off to the right was the circle of trees where the guide had taught the other visitors how to see their auras. Chiara had not needed to do this, as she had studied aura reading for years, but for her, the small clearing where the trees arced sharply left and right as if defining the perimeter of a tornado's winds had very different significance. She could feel the power of the place come up through her feet, and it swayed her as she stood there, in varying ways depending on where she stood. She meant to hit both of these spots again, and headed for the labyrinth while the others finished up, knowing they would be at it at least another half hour, playing with the props.

Pausing on the threshold of the small maze, she emptied her mind. She needed to see more clearly if she were to navigate the next few days. What clues could this walk give her, which she had so far been blinded to? She wanted to be open. She had to be.

There. She stepped through the redwood arch onto the first bricks, setting her mind in the direction of discovery. *What can I find here to help me on the outside?*

Her mind searching for answers to that question, she continued slowly along the light colored bricks, only vaguely aware of the fragrant breeze that whispered through the branches overhead. The call of a bird she did not recognize echoed through the trees off to the west. The murmuring voices of her crew underscored and punctuated her thoughts. After each step she paused, closing her eyes, letting whatever current impressions swirled around her settle in.

The forest stretches off into the distance for miles.

I sense the power coming from below. There. There. And there.

It calls me.

What am I missing?

She considered this last through several steps. What was she missing? She had her avocation, her crew, all the equipment she could use. She had determination in abundance. What then?

You don't have Hunter. Her lips pressed together in irritation. *If he can't see that I'm worth something to him, then maybe I don't need him.*

The concept settled in like snowflakes slowly landing in the ground, a small chunk at a time, bringing her to a halt. *I don't need him.* Her eyes snapped open. Before her stood the circle of tortured trees that held the strongest vortex in this compound. She did not bother to finish the labyrinth. She walked back out through the arch and crossed to the Aura Spot, taking position right in the middle. She extended her arms, hands palms up, and closed her eyes. *Lead me where I need to go.*

Her body shuddered as waves of dizziness washed over her. She fought to remain upright, and then gave in to the impulse that drew her head forward. She did not look, but she knew she was not vertical any more, much closer to a forty five degree angle to the ground, but she did not feel like she was going to fall. *Where is it?* She asked the forces that held her. *Take me there.*

She felt an impulse to lurch forward in the direction of her right hand, but was interrupted by the outcry from her crew. Yanked back into the conscious world, Chiara stumbled and caught her balance. She turned to see the cameras sat up and whirring in her direction. "You got that?"

"What the hell was that?" Artie just stared. "I thought you were going to fall flat on your face, but you didn't."

"No, I didn't." Chiara felt a rush of heat to her face, a little embarrassed to be the unwitting subject of the team's focus. She much preferred to be on camera on her own terms. "It's the vortex energy."

Janie, eyes wide, watched her with great interest. "A great demonstration of your point, though."

"Yeah." Chiara scuffed a foot on the ground. "So, did you finish with the house?"

"Something odd about it," Steve said. "But, yeah. Can't put my finger on it."

Janie giggled. "Steve fell off the ladder."

"Hey, I was demonstrating the properties, that's all." Steve hunched his broad shoulders and turned his attention to the equipment in his hand, as if it were the most fascinating thing in the world.

Chiara smiled. The 'properties' had showed her the direction to go. As soon as they finished here, she was ready to hike out cross country. She made sure the camera was set up and prepared to give the spiel that would become part of the permanent record. "All right, let me show you the fascinating details of the Aura Spot."

CHAPTER 15

LANE filled the black backpack with assorted objects, trying to decide what he would need for a whole day and night up in the mountains. So far he had a thick jersey hoodie, his enchanted laptop, two bottles of water and four double packages of Creamy Cupcakes.

You never knew when a serious stress attack would happen.

He sighed and set the backpack on the table. Only days until the formal ritual, and he was already nervous. This year was different than the last several, according to Daven, and each of the mages were expected to perform a part of the ceremony that would help align the vortexes with their usual outlets.

That left him scrambling to find something showy enough to prove to the old witches that Daven had not made a mistake when he chose Lane to become the clan's techno-mage and representative of humanity.

Even with the laptop Max had infused with the clan soil, making it, to the best of his understanding, an honorary elf, and by extension perhaps even Lane himself, he was not sure what he could do. Most of his skills involved finding things online, pulling off giant raids in the MMORPG games, making sure he could have food delivered in the event he and Crispy did not want to go out. What could he do to truly make a dent in this ritual to corral the wandering vortexes?

He could not think of a single thing.

"Crisp? Are you ready yet?"

His roommate's muffled voice came from the bedroom. "In a minute."

At least that was something. Once Lane had gotten Crispy to agree to attend the ritual, there had been much less reclusive behavior, and an almost positive attitude. *Jelly Bean and the elves aren't the only ones counting on this ooga-booga stuff to get themselves together.*

In reflecting on his role over the last several weeks, Lane realized that his affiliation with the elves had changed him as well. The coordination of the mages for the ritual required a close interaction he found strengthening. Someone else needed him. Someone else cared about him. Someone else depended on him.

Take that, all you people in my childhood who said I was effing useless.

And, as his grandmother had always complained, at least he was going outside to play.

Crispy finally appeared, wearing three layers of black clothing.

Lane frowned. "Is this a ninja operation and someone forgot to tell me?"

"No!" Crispy looked down at what he wore. "I just thought we might have to hide from that crazy journalist. I can blend into the shadows now."

"In black? I don't think so, Crisp. Shadows in the mountains are more in the grayish brown variety."

"Oh." Crispy's mouth turned down. "Well...."

"I'm sure it's fine. Layers are fine anyway. Don't worry about it." Lane shouldered his pack. "They'll tell us what to wear for the ritual anyway. So when we go back Friday we'll be all set."

"As long as they're not going to sacrifice anyone."

"Crisp! Why would you say such a thing?" Lane opened the door, held it for his roommate to pass through, and then locked it behind them. Their neighbor Tom must have heard them and stuck his head out his door to give them a hearty wave before going back to the baseball game that blared from his open apartment door.

"That's what rituals are about, right? If they don't have a virgin, maybe they'll just take whoever's the most messed up and whack them, right there. It'll purify the whole lot."

Lane could not believe what he was hearing. *Oh, wait. It's Crispy. Of course I can.* At least he was riding along voluntarily. "I'm sure you'll be fine, Crisp. It's not you I'm worried about."

Crispy's sharp gaze dissected him as they went around to the back of the building to climb into the truck. "Who are you worried about? Jelani? Astan? Daven? Elliun? Vez? Beckley?" When Lane did not respond immediately, Crispy continued down the list of elves until Lane finally cut him off.

"Dude! Get a grip, will you?" Feeling silly and selfish now, Lane gunned the engine, nearly choking it out in the process. It was not until they left the parking lot and headed west on Broadway did he admit he worried most about himself.

"You?" Crispy's eyes widened his jaw dropping. "How can you be worried about you? You're so…you can do anything."

Lane pulled up to stop at the red light and turned to see if his roommate was yanking his leg, big time. "What?"

"You can do anything. You have the protection of the elves and the magic laptop. You can even kill evil elf usurpers! And you're just…." He struggled for the right words. "You've always taken care of me, Lane. Even when I was at my most lost, you could always find me. Whatever life gives you, you always throw it back in its face. Nothing ever gets to you." A small smile came to him. "I want to be you when I grow up."

Lane rolled his eyes and growled. "Right. Lane the Conqueror, huh? Lane the Magnificent." He considered that a moment. "Though it does have a ring to it."

"*The* Lane," Crispy corrected.

That made him chuckle. "Yes, all right. I guess I'll think of something."

* * *

THE nerves along Lane's spine sent off warning signals. He plumped down on a thick log in the middle of the Circle's meeting bower, shivering even though it was midday under the full sun. While he loved his Jelly Bean dearly, and he respected Astan and some of the other Youngers, the old ladies of the Circle flat out gave him the creeps.

And there she was, the worst of the bunch. Djana, the woman who would be queen.

Even as he stared at the thin, wiry elf woman with the black hair, its gray streak nearly faded now, she turned her dark gaze on him from her place in the front of the 'room', as if she had read his thoughts. A twitch ran through him. The only good thing was that he knew she could not harm him. He was an official mage of the clan now. A technomage, thanks to his skills. And they needed him.

So take that, you old witch.

Now it was her turn to twitch. He grinned. She quickly looked away and addressed the gathered group.

"The solstice fast approaches, but the vortex energies seem to be even more disturbed than before as we come closer. We are concerned that we cannot wait until the appointed time, lest we risk some sort of disruption in the clan's health."

She and the other female Elders turned to Jelani, who waited off to the side with Astan. Elliun and little Kayli sat in the front row with Daven and Iris, who acted just like doting human grandparents.

Yeah, and like that's not odd, Iris practically being her best friend's mother in law.

Jelani came forward. "I've got to admit it's refreshing that you want to do something in a way that's different from the way it's always been done."

Lane translated that to: *If this had been my idea, you would have said it sucked.*

"On the other hand, this has been building for months now, and we're a week away from the solstice. I'd like to hear what indications specifically worry you. What make you want to move the schedule forward?"

"Haven't you sensed the volatility in the energy field?" Djana asked. "Especially in the last week. It's deteriorating quickly."

"I'm aware of it, yes, but the vortex energy has fluctuated for the last year. With the clan united again, we create quite a bit of energy of our own, remember. The mages are doing what they can to keep this balanced."

Jelani looked to Daven, whose face showed reluctance to quit playing with the angelic Kayli and join the group, but he did so.

"I'd have to agree with you both. There has been quite a struggle to keep control of the forces we cannot see, and some unknown variable has entered the picture in the last few days, this is true. But we're only talking another two days."

"But what's causing it?" someone demanded from the crowd. "Are we about to have another clan split? Is there destruction ready to fall upon us?"

Lane frowned and leaned forward trying to see who was trying to be the elf equivalent of the newscaster. The 'sky is falling' stuff was a bit much. The weather had been pretty much the same for the last several weeks, no earthquake type activity that he could remember. Could be that wave of new lumbering which had settled somewhere up in the mountain. He imagined the old trees would rumble a bit about that. What else might have changed?

Your pal the vortex hunter?

The more he thought about it, the more it made sense. Maybe a destructive energy came with them from New York? Or it could be the all the natural energies were clashing with the fake commercialistic drive of reality shows networks. Daven was still speaking, but Lane raised his hand.

"Yes, Lane? What insights come from the human world?"

Djana's eyes narrowed, as if Daven had said 'poisons' instead of 'insights'. But that was just like her.

"She might be all make up and hair color from a bottle on the outside, but my research shows she really does have a second sight of some sort, a sixth sense. Her abilities may be interacting with the vortex in some way. She's...." How to describe the woman? "She seems to be in a lot of pain, not physical, but something in her history. Maybe she's projecting some of that onto your whirly thing. Could she, unknowingly, be stirring it up to a frenzy?"

Daven assumed his usual contemplative expression, while the elders chattered about among themselves. Finally, Daven held out a hand to quiet them.

"It is possible that this human's talents have contributed to the situation. Elves are not the only ones who have the power to affect natural places, as you well know. Latent tendencies can pass through generations. This woman's chaos could be a factor." He glanced at Iris. "Perhaps I should go see her."

Lane chewed his lip a minute, half wanting to rest on his laurels at this point, and half worried about what Daven might do. "As long as you don't tell her elves are real. I mean, I've finally got her talked out of it. I think. Or at least that if there are elves, they're not in this neck of the woods, so to speak. If you get her started again, who knows what she'll do?"

Djana glared at Lane, but to his surprise came in on his side. "Absolutely not. The woman cannot discover us. Exposure could mean the death of the clan, either from curious humans over-running our lands, or the possibility we could be forced to move away from the lands we've held for so long. You know what it did to us before, and we only went as far as Missoula."

"Yes, Mother. I know." Daven's tone was the one he used to calm a savage bear he met in the forest. She looked like she was going to snap at him for it, but he waved a hand in her direction and she sat down, a sour expression on her face.

Jelani looked around the room, pinpointing Kalinda and Rudra, also mages, though much lower key than Daven, or even Lane himself. "What do you think?" she asked.

Rudra shrugged and mumbled to the elf woman seated next to her, in her usual bid to be ignored. Kalinda, though, conferred briefly with the Younger Lokni, and spoke up. "We should keep to tradition. If Daven Talvi can calm the waters until the solstice, everything will be as it should. The winds speak to us, and they say all will be well."

Jelani thanked her and went on with the meeting. Lane found his mind wandering along the possibilities of the wind 'speaking' to anyone, a ridiculous thought. Even as much as he had been exposed to magic among the elves, and spent more than half his waking hours, and some of his sleeping ones, engaged in an ephemeral zone of bits and bytes in the online game that was so much less than real, he found it hard to believe that someone could commune with nature to such an extent. He had witnessed Jelani's power to heal broken trees and damaged stands of wood and grass. But he still could not believe the wind 'spoke' to them.

Fighting avatar scolding from his head, he tried to concentrate on what he was supposed to be doing. Good thing too, because then Jelly Bean turned to him.

"And what can we expect from the amazing technomage department?" she asked.

The sparkle in her eyes showed that she teased him, and for just a moment she looked like his dear friend the barista, before the cares and worries of being a queen settled on her shoulders. He owed more to her right now that just a joke between good old buddies. As her colleague and advisor, she was counting on him for something magnificent.

And he had nothing.

Crispy elbowed him and Lane yelped and stood up. "I'm ready to do whatever you all think I can," he said. Even as the words came out he realized how lame that sounded. Here was his opportunity to wow them, and he was practically begging for a cheat sheet. He cleared his throat, hoping he did not choke. "What I mean is, I will do whatever I can to support your ritual without getting in your way. Whether that entails generating effects, appropriate music, killing villains...."

He trailed off, as they stared at him blankly. *Not the right answers.*

For the past several years, he had been able to bring the magic laptop and sit in the back row, like he had in middle school chorus, singing just loud enough that he was part of the group, but not really expected to excel. It was not like he could make his computer harness the vortex energy. Since that was the particular purpose of the ritual this year, he did not have much he could do to help.

Though Daven smiled with mild encouragement, and Djana gave him the evil eye, it was Jelani's look of disappointment that cut him as she nodded and went on with the rest of the pep talk. One by one the others turned away, dismissing him too.

Not good enough, Donatelli. You're going to have to come up with some way to be useful, and from the front row, too.

He sighed and sat back down, already contemplating how many packs of Creamy Cupcakes and cups of tea it would take to fuel the revelation he needed to find.

CHAPTER 16

THE early morning chill sat heavy on these mountains like a thick beaded necklace. Strange that the nights would be so cool, and then by mid-afternoon the temperature would approach ninety degrees. Like the desert. Not like her beloved New York, where summer heat and humidity oozed off the pavement day and night, making it hard to breathe, sleep, or go anywhere that was not artificially chilled.

But I could get used to mountain air.

Set on her morning's mission to find an open vein of the vortex energy, Chiara inched forward, half depending on the little voice in her gut, half depending on the device in her hand, which gave her the readings she wanted to see. This was the physical evidence, right here in front of her. Half holding her breath, she knew it was so close she could taste it.

She nearly tripped over a log as she looked up from her reader and found herself face to face with a small boy.

"Hello," he said.

Chiara glanced over her shoulder to see if any of her crew were handy, but could not see them. She had been in such a hurry to get up this mountain that she had left them behind. When she turned back to the boy, he smiled at her, brown eyes dancing with mischief. She guessed he was perhaps seven or eight years old, at least dressed appropriately for the weather in a short sleeved jacket and long pants, though it wasn't the usual kids' uniform of smart aleck T-shirt and denim jeans. She could not really say what his clothing was made from. He did not seem frightened to meet a stranger.

"Hello," she finally said. "Are your parents here somewhere? You know there are wild animals in this part of the woods."

He stared at her a moment and then laughed. "Are you afraid

of wild animals, then?"

What a strange question.

A picture appeared in her mind of a huge grizzly bear, reared up on its hind legs, teeth bared, claws waving. She gasped. He stared at her, amusement in his eyes.

Had he sent that picture to her?

Was he telepathic? She wondered if he would 'hear' her.

Of course. They're dangerous.

Her response provoked a smile. "Only if you mistreat them." The slender boy moved a little closer, his rapt attention fixed on the device in her hands. "What's that?"

Impertinent little thing.

"You answer my question first. Are your parents close by?"

She scanned the woods around them for the sound of panicked footsteps searching for a lost or misplaced child but did not hear any. The last thing she needed was to be found in the woods with a missing child.

Although, if I found one that was lost, at least that would be good press.

He cocked his head and then nodded. "They're around."

"That's good."

The kid did not seem afraid of anything, least of all her. He went back to watching her equipment. *Are you taking pictures? Or are you measuring the energy of the Donoma?* He waved his hand in a spiral.

She blinked as his words appeared in her thoughts, sounding like those transmitted through a tin can and string telephone. *How do you know that?*

Delighted, his face split in a grin, and he reverted to verbal speech. "I guessed right! Max always says I can't read humans, but I can." He did a little celebratory dance.

Read humans? What an odd phrase. Was he a reader, like Chiara herself?

She turned her attention to the boy, seeing what she could pick up from him nonverbally. If he were closer, she could get a better read. "Want to see it?"

He glanced over his shoulder, and then dashed across the

distance between them, his hand extended. She gave him the device, knowing it would not tell him anything. The uninitiated could not understand the sophisticated machinery Chiara and her people used. It had taken her weeks of training to understand the intricate gradations of the magnetic levels. She let her fingers touch his as she handed it over, picking up a little electric shock of non-recognition. His would not be a touch reading. *But he can send and receive, both. How often do you find someone like that?* She looked around them at the forest, anticipating these anxious parents who did not appear.

Maybe he's one of those Indigo children. I've never met one of those before. That would be a fascinating study, too. After I get this Vortex show on the air, maybe I could do a follow up, interview the kid, his parents, maybe his doctor.

He crouched down, studying the device in tight fascination, trying every dial. "Max would love this," he murmured.

"Max? Is that your brother?" Chiara used his distraction with the device to walk around him in a complete circle, attempting to gather her usual quick read, impressions, emotional temperature, but she got nothing. Well, not nothing exactly, but not what she expected. At least with most people, she could feel her 'bubble' of emotional space contact the other person's 'bubble', but with this child, her space simply seemed to fade away into mist.

Maybe it's because he's a kid.

It was true that it was sometimes harder to read children because of their rapid fire and scattered thoughts. But she did not think that was it.

"Who's Max?" she asked, when he did not answer.

A guilty look from him was all the answer she got. He looked again into the woods in the direction from which he had come, and then back at the device. Swinging the front of it around the small clearing, he stopped in the direction of the northeast, the exact spot for which she had been looking.

"That's it, isn't it? You're looking for the vortex."

How the hell did the kid know that?

"You know about the vortex? Are your parents scientists or

something?"

His faint smile gave away no secrets. He stood up and handed the scanner back to her. "Of course I know about the vortex. Without it, we wouldn't live. That's why we have to have the ritual. To repair it."

Now what was this? Chiara could not help the burgeoning curiosity that spilled over her like a waterfall of the mighty Columbia. Who required a vortex to live? What could that possibly mean? And was it broken? Was that the source of all the new phenomena? She had to know.

"Look, I know your folks probably told you not to talk to strangers, so let me introduce myself. I'm—"

You're the TV lady. His interest mimicked an entomologist studying a newly discovered bug, eyes narrowing as they took in every detail of her.

She choked on her next words. She had totally lost control of this conversation. She took several deep breaths in, several out. *Try again.* "I do work on television, yes. I'm Chiara DeLuna. Have you seen my show?"

He laughed. "I don't see television. Television programming is pap for dull humans' minds."

A sting of insult hit Chiara right in her midsection. "What? Who told you that?"

"Nana Djana."

Nana Djana? Was that some PBS reading show? Where did this Nana banana woman get off telling people Chiara's work was 'pap'?

She growled. "And you're not a 'dull human', is that it?"

"I'm not human at all." He crossed his arms, seeming to enjoy their repartee. "And she wouldn't like you calling her 'Nana Banana'."

Chiara snorted. "Right. You're not human. Even though you look just like one. Two eyes, two hands, two legs, and a mouth." After a moment it was obvious he had no intention of changing his statement. With a deep breath, she glanced up at the tree branches blowing overhead, whispering among themselves. Were they mocking her for entertaining this ridiculous conversation?

"So what are you?"

"I'm Elliun. I'm an elf."

"You're an—" She could not say it.

"Elf. Right."

A sharp whistle sounded from behind him, causing the first look of panic she had seen since they met. A moment later, a large red-tailed hawk swooped down into the clearing to land on his shoulder, giving off a tremendous squawk. Elliun's face flushed, and his expression changed to one of exasperation.

"I can't believe you're helping him," he said to the bird.

Chiara watched, fascinated, as he caressed the raptor's head, and the hawk let him, clearly tolerating the affection. The boy certainly had an affinity for wild things. "So your parents are elves, too?"

"My father is. My mother's only half elf, but they let her be the queen anyway."

"Your mother's the queen of the elves." *Well, if the kid was jacking her around, he was certainly going all in.* At the same time, something in her memory jogged. *Queen Elf.* That novel by Lane Donatelli, he called it fiction and had set it in another area of Montana, but something resonated here.

"Sure. And that makes me the prince."

"I could see how that works out. Can I take your picture? I've never met a prince before." She dug with one hand for her camera in her pocket. No telling where this was going, but it could surely be a bigger story than some unwieldy energy vortex. There were elves, here in the real world? That would be bigger than Bigfoot, and much less smelly.

For the first time the boy appeared reluctant. He took a step back and shoved his hands in his pockets. "No. That wouldn't be a good idea."

More importantly, the hawk picked up the change in the child's demeanor and screeched at Chiara. His wings flapped and he came up into the air. It hovered halfway between them with its claws extended, as if ready to defend the boy.

Did she hear herself thinking? A boy alone in the forest who claimed to be an elf prince and had a pet hawk ready to scratch out people's eyes? An Indigo child? Unlikely as that was, it seemed more likely than elves.

It's true. His thought tasted reluctant and remorseful in her head.

If it was true, this might be her only chance. Regardless of what she believed, she put the video camera up to her eye, determined to get this on film.

"No!" the boy yelled.

The hawk came at Chiara, screeching and clawing. She stumbled backward, sure she was about to die, camera still in her hand. The hawk pulled up as she moved away from its charge. Somehow she managed to stay on her feet and keep her finger on the record button.

Through the camera lens she saw a tall, thin young man float into the clearing from the trees above. His skin was pale as the moon and his shoulder length hair was a shock of white. He eyed her with something akin to hatred. He then grabbed the boy by the shoulder and dragged him off into the woods behind them. The hawk continued to patrol the sky above the clearing, leaving her alone as long as she remained on her 'side', but swooping at her if she approached the place where the boy had stood. She was apparently not going to be allowed to follow them.

But I got it on camera.

She ran it back, just to make sure she really had something. *Who knew, maybe elves couldn't be filmed…like spirits….*

But no, there they were, the boy Elliun and his ghostly guardian. Could that be Max?

Could there really be elves in these woods?

Shaken, Chiara tucked her camera in her jacket pocket and started back the way she had come, wishing like hell one of the others had been there to see it. Then she would not feel quite so crazy. But if this panned out, she would be on top once again.

The thought spurred her onward and she practically ran down to meet her team.

CHAPTER 17

DISMAY? Terror? Horror? None of these words was strong enough, but all these feelings passed through Max as he realized Elliun had slipped away from his scrutiny one more time.

Max did not rely on his own ears this time, knowing the previous incident had been reported to the queen and received with a tender disappointment that broke Max's heart. He summoned the hawk Crispy Mendell and Astan had stolen back from the edge of death, the one that had fixed himself on the young prince in the wake of his disappearance as a newborn babe. The hawk would find him.

And find him he did. In the worst circumstances Max could imagine, speaking with the woman who had come to expose and interfere with the clan's use of the energy vortex.

What was Elliun thinking?

Sick to his stomach as he pondered the implications of this meeting, Max watched from a place hidden from view. He knew he should retrieve the errant prince, but there seemed to be no good time to interrupt without making the situation worse.

But it's bad enough.

What would Jelani say? If she had been upset with Max when the boy had simply vanished for an hour, coming home unscathed, he could only imagine what punishment she would heap on him for this transgression. Exposing him to humans was unacceptable. But hearing the boy revealing the existence of elves in the forest to that 'muckraking woman', or so the Lane called her, Max knew he had blown his assignment, perhaps for the last time.

Once the hawk had done his job, scaring the woman away, Max took the chance to fly down and get Elliun, removing him from danger as efficiently as he could. He dragged the prince back under cover of the trees, so angry he could not allow himself to speak, lest he completely eviscerate the child with his sharp words.

Internally, he reminded himself Elliun was yet a young *nian*, learning self control and the extent of the dangers in the world. These were the years when he was supposed to make the mistakes that would teach him lessons he needed as an adult. Max was supposed to be the one teaching him those lessons.

If he would ever let me.

Elliun remained silent as they went on into the forest back toward the clan lands and the tree house where Jelani would be found. Usually the boy was cocky, full of excuses, but not this time. *At least he knew he had really crossed a line. If only I knew what to do about it.*

"Max?" Elliun whispered when they were nearly home. "I'm sorry. I didn't know that would happen."

Max halted his headlong plunge toward home. "When you just ran off, you mean? You didn't know you'd encounter danger? Even though I've warned you hundreds of times that just such a case might arise?"

The boy sighed heavily. "There were no bears or wolves within a mile. It seemed—"

"It *seemed?* Like that white rabbit that killed all the knights before they could use the Holy Hand Grenade. Even Lane knew better. She might look harmless, but clearly she's not harmless at all. You knew that woman was looking for an opportunity to impact our lives and you opened your mouth and gave it right to her!"

Elliun hung his head. "I just thought…I don't know. Maybe that if she started thinking about something else besides the vortex, that she wouldn't be so likely to find what she was looking for."

"And what was that?"

"The place where the vortex is running loose."

Max scowled. "Well that wasn't the way to do it."

"I know that now." Elliun's expression, and the pain in his

eyes, showed his remorse. "So, what are we going to do?"

"I don't know."

Max felt anxiety, like long worms hungry for their next meal, crawling around in his gut. He really had no idea what he was going to do. Maybe if he had some time to think, he could find a way to tell Jelani and Astan what had happened. But he just was not prepared to do it now. He had to find a way to delay the announcement, even if he had to lie.

"Elliun, I don't want you to get in trouble today. You know your mother would be angry if she found out what happened. She's got enough on her mind right now with the ritual."

Elliun's eyes filled with tears. "Max, I'm so sorry! I didn't mean it!"

Max nodded. "Let me handle it. I'll find a way."

"All right." The boy threw his arms around Max's waist. "Thank you," he said. "Thank you."

Surprised, Max hugged the boy and then walked him home, leaving him at the door. He still had no idea how he was going to tell Jelani and Astan what happened. He knew he had to, and soon, but he knew who could help. He had to get to the city and fast.

* * *

"ARE you effing kidding me?"

Lane's shout was so loud that both Crispy and Max pulled back in alarm. Max covered his ears, thinking perhaps this was the wrong move after all. But the Lane seemed so wise in the ways of the human world that Max could think of no one better able to give him an explanation that he could take to Jelani and the Circle, without being summarily dismissed, or decapitated. Lane just had not taken the news well.

"Elliun told her he was an elf? And the prince? Holy mother of God. Now she'll dig herself in even deeper. Oy...." Lane groaned. "He's not going to tell Jelly Bean first, is he?"

"He said he wouldn't." Max shrugged.

Curled up in the corner of the couch, Crispy returned to

reading his book, a pastime interrupted when Max had arrived in his agitated state. "Chiara can't prove anything," he said quietly. "Some little boy lost in the woods who made a few wild claims."

Lane's jaw dropped open and he stared at his roommate. "That's the first thing you've said in weeks that made sense."

Crispy did not even look up. He just smiled as he was reading.

"Really?" Max said. "You think she might just give up on it because he's a child?"

Lane plopped himself down in the Cave and started tapping instructions into his computers. "Let's see what she's got, if anything." His fingers hitting the keys on each of the computers in sequence, his screens came to life with pictures. "She's such an egomaniac, she'll post almost anything if she thinks it'll get her ahead."

Max watched from a safe distance, almost afraid to get within arms' reach in case Lane had another outburst. A host of pictures passed by, almost too quickly for him to see, most of them of that woman, and pages of words he could not read at the speed they passed by. But the last was the most shocking and left them both speechless.

"We're so dead," Lane said, staring at the monitor of his third computer as a shaky, hand held video lasting perhaps fifteen seconds played over and over. It showed Elliun, the attacking hawk, and worst of all, Max flying through the air to rescue him.

It looked like him, but Max could not understand what was happening. His thin body just went up and down, up and down. "What is that?" Max said.

"That's you, my friend. She managed to catch you on tape somehow." Lane shook his head.

"Why am I leaping in circles?"

Lane lifted his finger off his computer mouse and the video stopped. "I was trying to see if there was some way we could prove it wasn't you, or that it was faked, or...." He sighed. "But it's definitely you, and Elliun, too. How long did she have the camera rolling?"

Max frowned. "It rolled nowhere. She had it in her hand."

"Right. Exactly." Lane smacked himself in the forehead. "I meant, how much could she have on her camera? Did she have it in her hand when she was speaking to Elliun?"

"No. She didn't take it out until the hawk came."

Crispy grinned. "See, I told you he was worth saving."

The adrenaline of his mad rush to Missoula wearing off, Max felt a little dizzy, and he grabbed the edge of Lane's desk for balance. *All this way and there was still no good answer that came readily to hand.*

"Hey, hey! Kid! Have a seat." Lane lunged for one of the chairs at their little dining table and pulled it over for Max. "When's the last time you ate something?"

"I don't know. Some berries in the forest."

"Crisp, make the kid a sandwich. He's about to pass out."

Crispy eyed Lane over the top of his book.

Lane eyed him back. "I'd do it, but I'm tracking down how much damage we've got to contain here."

The thin man placed his book, open to save his place, on the sofa and went to the kitchen, muttering.

"He does not have to feed me," Max protested feebly. "I have put you to enough trouble already."

"Yes, he does," Lane said. "It's good for him. He's been a little under the weather. Helping someone else will make him feel better." He turned his attention back to the screens. "Damn her. I should have known she'd be more determined. She must be desperate as hell."

He flipped through a number of other pictures, faster than Max could follow. He finally paused on what Max recognized as his email screen. "And there it is. The whipped cream on the sundae."

Max understood that particular human term, but saw no frozen dessert of any kind. "People can send you ice cream?"

"No." Lane actually laughed. "Wouldn't that be a treat? No, she's sent me an email wanting to get together. 'To compare notes', she says."

Devastated, Max put his head in his hands. "I have to tell them. Djana will use this to prove she was right, that I was the wrong choice for this position of trust. How can I?"

Crispy brought a plate from the kitchen, and sat it on the edge of the desk while he dragged out a television tray from the small closet nearby. On the plate was a meat sandwich, perfectly cut into quarters, the crusts of the bread removed, a handful of potato chips, and three strawberries, set out in a triangle. The smell of the meat made Max's stomach rumble, even though he had no idea what it might be. Crispy sat up the tray and placed the meal in front of him. "Want some milk?"

Max had not even opened his mouth before Lane interrupted. "Of course he wants milk. We've got to put some meat on those hollow bones. Go ahead, Max. Eat up."

Crispy scurried off to the kitchen to fetch the drink and Max surrendered to Lane's pointed stare, devouring every crumb on the plate and drinking the glass of milk, even though he did not care for its thick taste. He was in Rome, so he had no choice. That, he had learned from Lane.

"Jelani will understand," Crispy said, returning to his place on the sofa. "She cares about people who are not perfect."

"Exactly right," Lane chimed in. "She likes us, doesn't she? We're not even close to perfect."

His gaze focused on the email. "But I bet she thinks she's got something for sure now. What else did he tell her? Anything about the oogabooga ceremony?"

Max tried to think back. He had not heard the entire conversation, that much he knew, because they were already engaged when he had finally tracked down Elliun. What had he been saying? "He told her the vortex was broken. And…yes. He told her we needed the vortex to live, and about the ritual."

"Son of a Christmas monkey." Lane groaned. "Now she'll bring reinforcements."

That was a new word to Max. "Re-in what?"

"Reinforcements. More guys to back her up. Bet she's pitching her story to the network brass right now." A sigh escaped him and he reached for a nearby box of cupcakes. "But...."

"But what?"

"But that gives me just the idea of what your clan's technomage can do to save the day." A smile started on his lips and spread until it lit up his entire face. "Oh yes, I'll be your superhero, my friend."

Lane pulled up the magic infused laptop, hesitating a moment before he entered a series of commands. "And now, we delete."

He pushed the delete key and the video vanished from the screen.

"Yes, awesome!"

Crispy frowned. "You closed the browser window?"

"No. The enhanced computer took the direction to delete right through to paranormal headquarters. It's deleted from the network's server."

"So they can't show it to anyone?" Max asked, still in shock.

"Exactly. Let her prove how smart she is now."

A grumble came from Crispy's direction. "I bet the government already took a copy of it for the FBI."

Max looked at Crispy, curious as to what the letters meant, but afraid to ask because of the man's tone.

Lane scoffed. "No. Well. Maybe." He cursed under his breath.

Max returned to the point he was most concerned about. "What about the queen? We still need to tell her this, right?"

Lane nodded, but he had swiveled his chair back toward the computer bank already, headed off in a new direction of thought. "Oh, yeah. We'll tell her. I'll even go with you, don't worry."

A flood of relief washed over Max that he would not have to go alone. He would just have to make sure Elliun backed him up on whatever he and Lane said. "What are we going to tell her?"

Lane cackled, a sound that sent a chill up Max's spine. "We are going to tell her that you and Elliun tricked Miss Crazy Luna into revealing her plan to spy on the elves during the ritual at the full moon. Moreover, we are going to tell her that you did this working with me, because I needed to know how much she knew in order to prepare a holo-screen that will block everything the elves are doing from the sight of human eyes to protect the clan and the ritual from her and all her evil minions."

He turned to Max. "You've saved my ass. And now I'll save yours."

CHAPTER 18

BACK at the hotel, Chiara had not been able to resist posting some of her footage online, just to tease the potential show to the masses.

She had sent a more comprehensive bit along to her network boss and to Hunter, and waited on a response, figuring that would guide her in whether she needed one show or two to cover all this material. She and the crew had mocked up a rough version of the examination of the commercial vortex site, with its leveling circles, aura spot, Golden Door and especially the Mystery House, footage of their experiments and interviews with the site's owners interspersed with her own researched commentary. It looked pretty good. She sent a copy along to Dan in New York as well.

But the potential that elves existed in northwest Montana intrigued her. She set Janie and Steve onto the Internet, seeking out whatever evidence they could find of magical beings in the woods. Well, once she had gotten past the ribbing about cookie baking in the trees and lost pots of gold.

"Leprechauns have pots of gold, not elves," she had corrected. She opened the sliding door onto her balcony, taking a deep breath of the fresh air. *I'm sure going to miss that.*

Artie chuckled. "Oh, right, right. Elves have what? Anything worthwhile? Do they grant you three wishes?"

"Come on, guys!" Chiara fumed and stopped just short of stamping her foot. "This is real. I spoke to this child, and he did tell me these things. You saw the vid of the one that can fly!" When they all just stared at her, faces contorted with their efforts not to laugh, she just growled and stomped out of the room. "You wait. Dan will think it's great."

She went into her bedroom and grabbed her cell phone off

the nightstand. About to dial her boss in New York, she was startled when the phone rang. She looked at the number.

Hunter.

Her mouth dried up and her hand trembled. What did he want? Would he be giving her good news or breaking it off once and for all? She almost did not answer it, but caught the button just before it went to voice mail.

"Hello?"

"Chiara, honey. It's so good to hear your voice."

The warmth in Hunter's words was unmistakable, and sounded very much like him during the first weeks of their courtship. Chiara was flabbergasted at the change from their last conversation. "It's good to hear yours, too." She listened a moment to the others in the outer room, hearing them still mocking her. "Did you get my video?"

"I did. Some really great stuff. Have you run it by Dan yet?"

"I sent it to him. Haven't heard back." She plopped down on the bed, the springs giving off a troubled screech. "I'm sure he's taking his time."

"Elves? Who would have thought of such a thing? I thought all that sort of fantasy material came out of Eastern Europe. Or maybe Ireland."

More with the damned leprechauns. "Come on, Hunter. I thought if anyone would have some vision it would be you. This is me. You know me. I wouldn't get all excited about something built of paper mache' and pushpins. I saw this with my own eyes."

"All a matter of being in the right place at the right time." He chuckled. "You surely have the knack."

She tried not to bristle, glad they were not on video. Everything in her took those two statements as sarcastic, as belittling her, but she so wanted to believe Hunter was being genuinely complimentary. "It's one of my best qualities," she said halfheartedly.

Silence fell between them, more awkward the longer it dragged on. She wanted to ask whether he was taking her back. Reluctance to make any offer at all was clear in his hesitation. Just when she thought stress driven nausea would overtake her, he continued, a little more softly.

"Chi, when you get back to town, we should talk. This episode will be a big hit. You'll see. With your self confidence back in place, you'll be good again."

Not exactly what I wanted to hear, now was it? "Talk about what, Hunter?"

"You and me. I...maybe I was hasty. You know I'm not a patient guy. I should have trusted you."

More like it. Relief flooded over her. On the other hand, the one not holding the phone, curled tight as her fingernails dug into her palm. *Don't you dare throw yourself at him and beg, Bonny Lang. Don't you do it!*

She did not know whether it was the sudden sting of her nails or the reminder of what she would go back to if she did not succeed with this spot, but she managed to keep her cool. "How's the, um, the investigation going on that old church in Tioga County?"

"You know, hun, I haven't had the heart to go back out there without you. Let's make that the first thing you do when you come back, all right? We'll work together. It'll be great." The sound of a phone ringing went off somewhere in the room behind him. "Hey, I've got to go. Let me know what Dan says, will you? Take care, and don't go falling off a mountain, huh?"

"I'll try." She held the phone to her ear for many long seconds after he hung up, thinking he almost sounded like his old self. She had done it. This story would absolutely make her land right back where she needed to be. *Thanks to you, little elf child.*

Janie stuck her head in the bedroom, pausing a moment to study Chiara's face. "You okay?"

Chiara sniffed. "Yeah. Fine."

"Good. Cause Dan just paged me. He wants you to call. Now."

"Will do, thanks."

She waited until Janie left the room. Then she took a deep breath and speed dialed Dan. *Here's one for all the marbles, Chiara babe.* He picked up on the second ring.

"Is that you, Chiara? I want to make sure it's really you and not some kind of practical joker. Because I know you wouldn't try to punk me. I know it. Not you."

Chiara blinked, taken off guard by what seemed to be an attack. Not what she had expected at all. "What are you talking about, Dan? Did you get my footage?"

"You bet. What is it now, The Blair Elf channel? I haven't seen such shoddy work since—"

Her backbone snapped into place. "Just you wait a minute. I sent you what I had, what I filmed on the fly on my cell. That's not all there will be when we're done."

"What else are you going to have?" It was his two antacid voice. That wasn't a good sign.

"I'm going to have proof, Dan. That video was just acknowledgment that I'm on the right track. I've got the vortex site show just about rough edited, and we can send that back for production to get started. Then I'm moving up into the woods to get this elf culture on film. I don't know how long I'll have to wait, but according to what the elf said—"

"The lost kid in the woods?" A heavy dose of disbelief came over the line.

"Damn it Dan, did you watch what I sent? These beings controlled the animals around them, and one flew out of a tree. Flew. Like a bird. No strings, no parachute, no nothing." She growled in frustration. "Just fasten your belt, all right? It's coming. I promise."

"It better be." He paused, wearing an odd expression. "If you've really got this, Chiara, I think I can guarantee you a nine p.m. slot. Better than the eleven, huh?"

In television advertising speak, this was fantastic. She knew enough to know that. "I've got it. We'll nail this one, and northwest Montana will never be the same."

"I'm counting on you, doll." He was gone a second later.

What a jerk. First, she was pummeled and then bribed, like an abused woman. What did he think she was? "Not for much longer, Dan," she muttered. *Not for much longer at all.* If she pulled this off and became a star, she would leave the network so fast his head would spin. She would be able to name her own ticket wherever she went next.

Now that thought she liked.

She might have to tree sit out in the woods for days to catch the elves unaware, like deer hunters did their prey. But she would do it, even if she shivered through the nights and sweated through the days. *No stopping until the job's done.*

Braced by the two conversations, she washed her face in the small bathroom and came back out to face the team. *Time to get this show on the road.*

* * *

DAVEN Talvi, his appearance cloaked from human eyes, slipped inside the open balcony door while the blonde woman talked on the phone. Her emotion filled the room, practically choking out the air. Daven moved quickly to the right of the door, avoiding the floating curtain that could reveal his presence if it caught on his body, and took up a place in the corner where he could listen to her, and to those in the other room.

Her companions spoke among each other in low tones, but critical of her, as though her judgment was somehow impaired. Daven was pleased to hear them limiting their discussion to the commercial Vortex site by the highway, at first, but then his attention was caught by Chiara's two conversations, especially when she mentioned the 'elf culture' and then the child in the woods.

Does she mean Elliun? Sweet Lady of the Forest!

His heart racing, Daven fought to remain static, calm enough to maintain his cloaked appearance. Her desperation was far worse than Lane had said. She was single mindedly focused on only one thing, herself. Every shred of her being indicated that she would sacrifice every member of the clan in order to raise herself in some other person's estimation.

I know not who might be on the other end of that telephone call, but they must be extremely important. How can I show her that she has value other than by exposing us? How can I convince her not to do this?

She stepped out of the room and Daven heard water running. While she was out, he seized the opportunity to take several tied bunches of healing herbs from his pocket and placed them in various hidden spots around the room. It was all he could do for now. She needed more curative treatment than he could provide in this open environment. His mind was also troubled by the revelation that this woman had seen, even spoken with Elliun. What impact would that have on their clan?

Did Astan and Jelani know this? Why hadn't he heard yet?

She returned to the bedchamber and suddenly froze. Her head cocked and she scanned slowly around the room, stopping to focus on a spot near where Daven stood, though she did not look right at him. Her mouth opened as if she was going to speak, but nothing came out.

Daven sent calming thoughts at her, knowing that if she called out to the others, he could cause more damage than had already been incurred. *She really is a sensitive, as Lane said. But this is not the moment. I'll catch up with her another time, when she's alone.*

"Who's there?" she whispered, her face pale.

He held perfectly still, hardly breathing.

A young woman stuck her head into the room. "Chi, you coming? I have some research I want to show you."

Chiara hesitated just a moment, and then visibly shook it off. "I'm coming," she said. With a final look around the room, she walked out with the other woman.

Daven breathed a sigh of relief, wasting no time in making his escape out the open door. For a moment he thought she might close the door before he could get out. Then he would have yet another issue to face. But now he needed to get back to Jelani as soon as he could. They might even have to change their plans for the ritual, to protect themselves. As much as he loved his grandson, this time he had gone too far. *His mother's rebellious streak may have finally done us in.*

CHAPTER 19

THE drive up Highway 93 seemed to take forever. Lane knew it was because he did not want to be going there, certainly would not have wanted to be in the firing line when Jelani found out what had happened. But he promised Max. After all Max had done for him, he could hardly refuse.

Crispy, on the other hand, had actually perked up, and carried on a spirited conversation with Max, the three of them crowded together in the front seat of the ancient red pickup.

There had to be some way that this could be turned into a positive. Sure, it would have been better if the woman had never known about the clan and where they could be found. But it was done now. All they could do was corral the damage and move on. Like their broken energy pit.

Besides, I should be able to distract Jelly Bean with that whole 'the vortex is out of control' thing, which has to be more important than assigning blame for this slip up. Right?

He sighed, hoping this was true.

They almost had Max cheered up and confident again by the time they parked the truck and walked up the hill to the clan lands and Jelani's place. But the tree house door opened before they even knocked.

That's a bad sign.

Jelani stood there, Kayli in her arms, eyes narrowed as she looked at the three of them. Daven stood behind her, face solemn. "Let's hear it," she said. "Elliun already told us his side."

Lane felt Max, who had been at his shoulder, pull back a little, hiding behind him. "Now Jelly Bean, let's not fly off the handle before Max can even explain." He pushed his way inside, cognizant as always of the collapse potential for this odd space time warp that was the continually growing inside of Jelani's house inside an old fir tree. Magic, it was, that held open this space. It was important to believe. Or else....

If you believe, clap your hands, everyone clap your hands! Hurry!

Max and Crispy filed in dutifully behind him, taking the chairs Jelani indicated. Lane glanced at Daven, wondering if he was here to break the ice. But he just looked sad. Elliun sat near the empty fireplace on a carved wooden chair, a rebellious look boiling in his eyes.

Lane hesitated before he took his usual chair and then decided he would rather be eye to eye with Jelani. He stood to speak to her. "Max is really upset about what happened, Jelly Bean. He told us—"

"I want him to tell *me*." Her eyes flashed. She pinpointed Max with that hot gaze.

Max looked at Lane, a quick shot of panic appearing in his eyes. "I should have kept the prince closer to me, and not let him out of my sight. When I realized he was gone, I did find him as soon as I could—"

Knowing Max expected him to do something, Lane took the opportunity to interrupt. "Look, the kid's home, the damage is done, and there's a silver lining here I think we're missing."

What was that silver lining again? I had it back at the house. His brain raced to catch up with his tongue.

"I'd love to hear it," she said.

He scrambled to pull out anything he could think of. "Now we know exactly how much she knows. Or what she thinks she knows. Won't it be easier to divert her from one place instead of her chasing all over the woods stumbling over elves every inch of the way?"

Yeah, that sounded good.

"That's not the point. Max—"

"That *is* the point. What's happened isn't Max's fault. He told me how Elliun has been getting less and less respectful of his orders and suggestions, and he's wandered off more than just this once." Seeing Jelani about to burst into words Lane hurried on, talking a little louder to block her out. "Elliun's the one who spilled the beans here, despite all that everyone has told him about talking to strangers or outsiders. So, yeah, there's going to be consequences here, and he needs to share them."

"On the other hand, you've got to realize that you have a growing boy here. He's going to want some freedom and he will get it, with or without your approval. He's a damn lucky kid to have two parents and a whole clan that loves him and wants him to be well, not like me when I was growing up, or like Crisp, or hell, like you, Jelly Bean. Elliun has every advantage here. But all that comfort and security just gives him a strong place from which he's going to try his wings. Right?"

Lane caught a quick look at Daven, whose lips had finally turned upwards in a small smile. *He approved. Half the battle done. Score!*

But that was not his biggest obstacle. She had not bent yet. Still rocking Kayli, who appeared to have gone to sleep despite the agitation in the room, Jelani walked into the nursery. After laying down the baby, Jelani came back with her arms crossed tight. "That doesn't change the fact that Max—"

"Max. Max. Max. Max. Okay, I see what's happening here." Lane took a deep breath, ready to launch into a deceptive tirade. *Max better appreciate this.* "You want to blame Max because some little voice in your head tells you that the Circle was right all along, that Max wasn't good enough to tutor your son. Even though they don't really care about sons, since you weren't supposed to have one in the first place. Remember that? Or how they didn't necessarily want you because you were different?"

Jelani started to interject, but he pitched his voice like a freight train that kept on rolling.

"Max is a perfectly capable individual in any circumstance. Just because he's not like all the other elves doesn't make him any less useful. I mean, if you think that, then you must believe the foster parents who thought Crisp and I would never grow up to do anything meaningful."

Before she could say that Lane had not done anything particularly meaningful, if you didn't count being the best warlock tank this side of Kansas, he blazed on. "And I'm a technomage!"

He gestured at Max. "This kid has grown up before our eyes, lived through an elf civil war or two and now he's proving that he is a great teacher to your boy because, like you, like us, he thinks out of the box. He isn't one of the Circle's parrots. He's going to be a great leader of your clan someday, and so is Elliun, because of him. You should be proud."

Jelani's mouth opened, and then closed. After a confused, silent moment, she turned to Max. "I…I am proud of what Max has done. I…." She looked like there was more she wanted to say, but she was not sure where to go.

"Okay. Good. If we're past that, do we have some tea? Because it's been a long day."

Lane took the chair at last, and spared a glance for Max, who just stared in open admiration. *Ah yes, minions. It's good to have minions.*

"These thoughts I, too, have shared," Daven added. "The world is changing, and the clan must change with it." Turning away from the queen so she could not see, he shared an amused expression with Lane.

Jelani went to the cold box and brought out some slightly chilled tea, which she poured into glasses for everyone but Elliun. She sent him to his room to write lines, an activity they all knew Elliun hated. Or if they had not known it before then, the wailing and complaining that came from the bedroom thereafter certainly convinced them.

"Maybe he should spend more time with you and Astan, too," Jelani said to Daven, joining them at the table. Max's face fell.

"Not because I think you're not doing a good job," she added quickly. "But because Lane's right. He is getting older, especially by elven standards, and he will learn much more from a diverse group of teachers. Like is said, it takes a village."

"You've got to factor in that he's in a well protected environment here," Lane said. "He should have the chance to experiment and grow like the other elflets."

He did not add that there were plenty of kids four and five years old across the country who ran loose on the streets even in big cities without this kind of supervision. He had been one. *Didn't make it right.*

"Maybe." She smiled. "It's different when it's your own child, Lane. After all we went through when he was born, you know."

Lane just nodded. The less said about those days in the past, the better. "Hey, and it got Crispy out of the house. So it's not all bad."

That switch of topic let Lane off the hook, as Jelani, Max and Crispy started talking about some sort of animal issue at the Wildlife Rehab center where Jelani and Crispy both volunteered. Lane sipped his tea and let his brain turn to the possibilities for defeating the Looney woman's plans. He had a pretty good idea how he could do that, by holographic projection, but he would have to make sure his projection had some substance to it. She seemed fairly determined. A mere ephemeral wall might not stop her.

But I've got elf magic working for me. If it can make delicious cookies, why can't it make a Great Wall, too?

CHAPTER 20

HIS conscience stung from the dressing down he had given himself the day before.

Even though Lane had kept Jelani from delivering one, Max found it hard to hold his head high as he marched with the dark robed others along the barely noticeable path to the place of the ritual, a spot on the Whitefish River just south of the lake, a place partly hidden from outsiders by a thick fence of Douglas firs.

Elliun slouched along by his side, only partly chastised by the chewing out his mother had given him. Max knew better. Jelani had been sidetracked by her concern over pulling off the intricacies involved in coordinating the ritual. Once everyone necessary was on hand, they decided to go immediately to be in place before dark.

The Mages who made up the *Idellan*, the balance of power, went first, each adorned in handmade baubles and woven flower chains that suited their particular calling. Daven Talvi held the arm of elder *neris* Rudra, who commanded power of the waters. After her close escape from death in the most recent rebellion several years before, she had become increasingly paranoid and reluctant to share any of her knowledge, though Max knew the Circle had become more insistent that she do so. Daven kept up a running commentary into her ear. Perhaps that was part of his way to charm her into compliance and persuade her into choosing a successor.

Tall, nondescript Lokni of the gray eyes walked quickly along, a braided crown of fragrant herbs on her head. This would be her first ritual as an anointed mage of the clan. Her tutor, Kalinda was close behind for added support. With the Blessing of the Lady of the Forest, Kalinda had reluctantly stepped aside as Mage of the Air, sending Lokni to study the ways of the *Intalus* at the otherworldly *Santwarja* with those Others who had passed beyond. She had spent many weeks there, but emerged thin and competent, gradually working herself into her powers. Whether she had mastered them would be tested today.

Lane Donatelli had left them at the fork in the path, proceeding west to stake out the place they expected this Chiara to be, his infused laptop being used to generate a special protective to keep the curious humans from interrupting what the elves must do here.

Max did not understand the whole process, or why Lane kept muttering something about the bus that could not slow down, but he knew Lane was satisfied that this task would complete his part of the ritual. Lane would be watching and participating at the ritual site through a particular magic called Skype, which he said would project a hologram of him in the middle of the group, so he would still be part of the service.

He had looked particularly magnificent to Max's eye, wearing a long purple robe and cape he said he purchased from a magician's supply shop, without the odd pointed purple hat with yellow stars painted on it. Crispy insisted that it be left at home for reasons Max did not understand. He personally thought it made The Lane look magical.

It was hard to explain humans.

Crispy, too, walked in quiet companionship along with Max and Elliun, seeming not to notice the tension between them and the royal family. He carried the small device through which Lane would project his essence, if all went well. His footsteps were nearly as light as those of the elves, who glided along the surface of the ground but that was because he scarcely weighed as much as a doe. Max glanced behind, with a hint of anxiety, hoping that the procession did not leave a trail that could be followed by anyone, particularly the investigator.

But I can't worry about that now. I have to keep Elliun safe. It's my last chance to prove I'm worthy of this task.

"Look, it's Hawky!" Crispy whispered, pointing overhead.

Sure enough, the hawk accompanied them on the excursion,

swooping in to land on Crispy's arm when he held it up. The deadly claws held on to the man's thin wrist, fortunately encased in a thick hoodie, and he regarded the parade with a hunter's disdain.

The general atmosphere felt like that of a party for the younger half of the troupe, but the Elders definitely projected a sort of worry and concern. Max tried to keep his mind clear. That seemed to serve him best in magic of any sort. Any sorts of negative thoughts you carried tended to clutter up your results, no matter what the intentions were.

The ragged marching group went deep into the forest to the place where the river bent in the shape of an elbow, taking up their places in concentric circles on both sides of the bank, leaving Daven and Jelani on a small outcropping of rock in the center of the river. Then all fell silent, even the very young, as they let the smell of the wind and water fill their lungs. The feel of the damp, cool air and the strength of the earth under their feet settled over them.

Max breathed deeply, letting his mind go, letting his muscles relax, thinking only of the other elves and humans around him and how they were part of him and part of his world, even if they might not be related by blood or relationship. A light seemed to bloom inside him, and he encouraged it, knowing the others would feel the same. Soon they would all be connected, one to the other, by psychic coils and strings of the energy that coursed through the ground beneath them. It would be similar to the gathering of elves that changed the course of their war with Bartolomey, the one where Max had shown Lane the different colors of the auras and bonds that attached all the elves to each other when they worked in harmony. It always felt so good, not just until the ritual was over, but for days and weeks after.

Maybe it would clear away the hate Jelani and Astan feel for me after what I did.

He caught the negative thought, purely coming from his own guilt, as neither of those elves had said as much, and removed it from his mind, dragging his attention back to the present moment as Daven raised his hand. Though he was the image of light, he wore all black, even a black cape, as if incorporating his opposite. When he began to speak, Max almost expected to hear the deep, powerful voice of the dark character from the Lane's star fighting game. But it was not so.

"We gather here because we are called by the energies within the earth, those life forces which sustain us as we sustain them. For so many years our clan lived in strife, decimated, and the *Donoma* was weak as well, unable to uphold the life we needed."

"Now we have lived several years as a whole clan, and we have done it well. Our energies have grown and become strong. The *Donoma*, however, has not been concurrently healed along with the breaks in the clan. We are called to give regulation to the forces below, so that they may resolve their own inner conflicts and serve us well."

He turned to his right. "To complete this undertaking, we have summoned all the mages of our people to work together and they have come as bidden. Each shall have a hand in this restoration. The balance shall be re-established."

He held out his hand to the right, where Rudra waited, her usual dark standoffishness falling away as she lit up with the magic within. She walked forward into the river up to her knees and then slowly lifted her arms. Water rushed up to embrace her, bubbling and fizzing like in the rapids further downstream. When she was surrounded by an energetic pillar of water, she tossed her arms skyward. Water shot up in a fountain, coming down over the entire clan like rain, a small baptism with the power of her water connection.

"May the waters sustain us and absorb the energies of the ground to channel their ways ever more to the service of all who depend on it for their life."

When the last drops had fallen, she seemed to lose the enthusiasm that had snapped through her, and several of the Youngers quickly moved to help her back onto the riverbank. When she was once more ensconced in her place, Daven held out an arm to the left, and Lokni moved forward in her robes, ready to perform her first major enchantment for the clan.

She stood for a moment on the bank of the river. With a circular wave of her hand, she transported herself on the air's currents to a place two elves' height above them all. Her voice shook at first, but as she connected with the sustaining forces her voice grew stronger until it echoed through the glade.

"May the sweet wind that brings us the air we breathe, that feeds our plants and trees, that smoothes our way and clears our heads come now to the aid of the energies of the earth, helping bring it back into balance."

She swirled her right hand and a vortex of wind, a clear funnel cloud, mostly sensed, not seen, formed right above her. She directed it downward, straight into the earth. A slight spray of dust fanned out over the gathered, but nothing that hurt them. Max felt the power of the coiled air shake the ground under his feet before arcs of the *Donoma* burst out and flew upward. Maybe this would be just what the clan needed. Then they could move back to their normal lives.

* * *

LANE waited at the edge of the forest between Chiara the Loon and the place where the ritual was set to take place.

While he had not been completely honest with Jelani, he had not misled her in any way that mattered. Once he had started thinking in the 'us versus them' mentality, he realized he could use the power of the computer to generate and project images. He could combine it with the magic bonded to it to generate and project images into the real world that would block the paranormal team from knowing where the ritual was or being able to find it.

This was not a new idea by any means. He had seen it in dozens of movies. But he certainly had never done it himself, and not on this scale.

Can't be that hard after what I did to bring old Xiomar from WoW into this world. Well, you wouldn't think so, anyway.

Lane found himself a relatively dry and comfortable spot

before whipping out the camp chair he had brought along. The chair was extra large and even had a cup holder where he could place his thermos of tea. Opening the laptop he started the program. He would place the computer on the ground where it would be able to draw from the clan's land. Besides, after all the Creamy Cupcakes he had consumed in his life, he just did not have much room on his lap anymore.

The last time he was up here, when they brought Max back home, he had taken some videos of this particular area. All he had to do was loop the video so that he could screen out an entire section of the woods from real time viewing and pray, or hope, that the projection would block it long enough until the ritual was complete.

All right, let 'er rip.

Lane set the parameters of the program he wanted to roll and closed his eyes, making that wish, just as hard as he had ever wished blowing out candles while growing up. *Never got many of those wishes, though, did I? That Mom would quit drinking or be less crazy? That I could stay a whole year in one house? That I could have a real family?*

Though the last had come true, eventually, not the way most people pictured it. His 'family' was comprised of a mentally broken foster brother, a former barista who was half elf born, her extended elf family, and his roommate's former therapist, and Max. The thought of that poor kid came to him unbidden. He was a real bright spot in Lane's life and he was family now, which is why Lane had to stick up for him with Jelly Bean. That's what brothers do for each other.

Concentrate, damn it. If you don't get this right, those old witches will eat your liver or something. Turn you into a newt for real this time.

He bent down with a grunt and set the running computer on the bare dirt. It immediately whirred into a higher gear, and he could sense it was doing 'something'. Now he had to see if it was doing what was needed.

"Hear, o elf clan of the Bitterroot, hear your technomage at work holding up his end of the bargain. Presto chango, Shazzam, Abracadabra, A la peanut butter sandwiches, hickory, dickory, dock, um, Shazbot! Make it so!"

Having exhausted his repertoire of magic incantations, he stood up and then moved around in front of the computer projection. Sure enough, his chair and everything else he brought was completely out of sight. All he could see was the forest in its pristine condition the day before, the river babbling away right smack in the middle. Although he could walk through it, no one else would be able to, not until he released the picture. So now all he had to do was wait. He settled into his chair and took a long sip of his tea, fingers only slightly itching for a keyboard under their tips. He could manage for an hour. He hoped. Meantime, he could electronically project himself into the herd for the rest of the ritual.

Just remember. It's good to be a mage. It's good to be a mage.

* * *

CHIARA and her team began covering all the areas she had mapped earlier in the afternoon, her sixth sense telling her something was taking place.

Some of the trees looked a little unfamiliar, not exactly as she remembered them, but she chalked that up to nerves. The sun streamed down warm on them like summer honey, bringing out the best of the natural world around them. She could imagine what this place was like in winter, but for now, it was one of the most beautiful spots on earth. The wind whispered to her, telling her secrets she almost understood, but the words would float away just as she was beginning to unravel them. It was all right. She knew she was on the right path.

Each armed with a video camera with enhanced audio, they climbed into pre-arranged trees, almost like they were hunters waiting for unsuspecting deer to come by. Not knowing how long they would have to wait, each had carried a backpack with water and non-crunchy snacks, their cellphones loaded and ready to send a message as soon as anyone spotted anything.

Chiara's tree branch was a little lumpy, and it was not long before she wished she had brought a pillow to sit on. Annoyed with herself for letting her personal comfort come before a story, she cleared her mind and went into what she called psychic communing mode.

Greetings to free spirits everywhere. We come in peace. We only wish to share your world for a brief time.

Spirits would not understand the need to make a living, right? She could tell half the story, hoping to get her message across without confusing them.

A jolt of energy came right up through the tree into her body, shaking and spinning her. She grabbed the branch and would have dropped the camera if it was not strapped to her wrist. *The vortex!* They had to be close.

She pulled the camera quickly to her eye, ready to shoot as soon as she saw anything. But nothing happened. She closed her eyes and reached out with her emotions, her heart, sensing the interplay of powers just beyond her reach. Had she missed the spot? She came to the spot the child had pointed out, she was sure of it. The river was just there, the bend in it right in front of her. It was the most sensitive psychic place in the whole region. It had to be where the ritual was taking place.

Then why don't I have anything on film?

Another jolt of a vortex nearly knocked her from the tree, and this time she just held on for dear life. The splatter of rain fell on her and disappeared. The wind blew past her, hard enough she had to close her eyes to keep the dust from them. She grabbed her cellphone.

"Any of you seeing anything?" she demanded.

"Not me, boss. Just a bunch of birds taking a bath in the creek."

None of the others had anything either. But she knew. Something was happening just out of her sight. She shimmied down the tree, tearing her eighty-five dollar slacks, and walked first left and then right to see what trick of light might be hiding the truth from her. She could not find anything. She was stymied.

* * *

DAVEN stepped aside and Jelani came to the front of the small central space, feeling so much a part of the forest in a medium green gown that brushed the ground with its hem. "We come together to set our world right again, not because we are falling apart this time, but because we are doing so well that we have overwhelmed our source," she said. "We do this as one people, with all our breaths, with all our air, with all ourselves, with our deep roots attached to this land."

She looked around, feeling a connection with each one of these shining beings who were now hers, knowing some of it was magic, but some of it was completely real, too. Astan waited across the river with Elliun and Kayli, his face proud and his stance supportive of her. They had finally made their own way to be the leaders of this small clan, and it had rewarded them in so many ways. She was not always as thankful as she should be. This ritual was an opportunity for her to give back, too.

"We all experience the energy that comes from the earth to sustain us, just as if we were the strongest of these fir trees around us. We receive the gift of life, air, water, earth, fire and light that come to us, as they do to all the life around us. They keep us balanced. Let the energies come into you now. Channel it well and we will be the instruments of this balance."

She looked to the right of the place where Astan stood and saw the misty form of the Lady of the Forest. Jelani had encountered her many times since coming to live with the clan. She was a definite presence, though not always seen clearly. Daven had explained that the Lady was almost a mirror image of Jelani as the queen, her entry and proxy in the spirit world, who helped strengthen Jelani's magic powers but who took nothing away. Jelani held her hands out to the Lady, who approached her across the waters, floating above them, hardly seen. When they touched each other the gathered elves gasped, a long reverent moment passed, and then a rumble began deep in the earth under their feet. The power of the movement was stronger than Jelani expected and for a moment, a little thrill of fear ran through her. Had they gone too far?

I would never let you come to harm, child.

Jelani let the reassurance of the Lady settle into her, waiting for the energy to rise from the earth, which it finally did, coming up her legs, her spine, freezing her in place with its power, working to the crown of her head, where it burst forth in dizzying twirls of light and wind. The others around her felt the same thing. She could see how they swayed and their same look of release as the energy burst through them, not leaving a physical sign, but changing them just the same.

When the excess energies had been released up into the sky, she bid the Lady thanks and sent her on her way again. Daven, as mage of light, sealed the circle binding the clan together with a huge spiral of light that began on the outside of the group and curled in on itself tighter and tighter until it circled just Daven and Jelani. They exchanged fond looks in that small enchanted circle, beyond those petty jealousies that had saturated their early days. Now both belonged to the clan.

When the last light had faded from Daven's blessing, only one other mage who needed to perform her duties to complete the ritual, but she was nowhere in the gathered crowd. Would Veraena even come, considering her sad history? They had welcomed her, as they had all the others, even though she had sided with Bartolomey during the war. Instead, she had chosen to wander free from clan. The pain of seeing the remains of her family could be too much for her. But what if she did not do her part?

"Do you think she's coming?" Jelani asked quietly.

Daven cocked his head, listening with some part of his body beyond his ears. "She's here."

As if on cue, the cloudless sky was split with a crack of thunder, and a dozen fireballs the size of melons shot up from a point over to the right, arcing across the river to fall nearly to the ground before exploding in a burst of cold ash. Silence accompanied the spectacle, and continued even after it was done. *A reverent and fitting end to their effort.*

That was until Djana stepped forward, taking Kayli from

Astan's arms.

"One last blessing, and then we may accept the Lady's gifts and return to our homes," she said, coming up to the end of the river, the other *neris* of the Circle on her heels.

The muscles in Jelani's neck tightened in protest. She had been against this part of the ceremony. She begged Astan to back her, but in the end he convinced her that whatever else happened, this would not hurt anything. He was her mate, and Kayli's father. She had to trust him on this one. She just bit her lip before something horrible sprang out.

Djana likely knew she had a short rope to hang from on this one, so she wasted no time. "We come today in the wake of the balancing of the vortex to consecrate our next queen. We saw what happened last time when we let the queen leave at birth without being made part of the clan, thanks to her human father."

You want to talk about my human father in that tone of voice? I'll give you—

Astan put a hand on Jelani's arm, and she cleared her throat in irritation. "I know, I know."

"We offer this young *neris* Kayli, born of Astan Hawk and the queen of the clan, Jelani Marsh, and ask the mages to accept and consecrate her as our next queen, in the tradition of our people. The queen is always next born from the queen before her, and we ask that she be blessed and that she rule in peace for many years to come."

Djana held the child up for all to see, and they murmured a blessing in response. Jelani thought it was ridiculous, as Kayli was hardly two years old and would not need to rule for many years to come. But it kept peace in the family. And that was worth all the lip biting it took.

As soon as she could, without being rude, she broke in. "May the Lady bless us all. Join now in peace, letting the gifts of this day fill your hearts and build our world, keeping us safe."

Anticipation swept through the gathered elves as the climax of their ritual approached. They drew closer to each other, touching or holding hands, each building a network of strength with the ones next to them, an interdependent web of life. Jelani exchanged glances with Daven and he released the light that had earlier spiraled in on them. It spread over the clan members like an illuminated umbrella. The ground rumbled. Then a rush of energy erupted. Happiness and strength burst upward, bathing the elves and their guests in a warm revitalizing ambiance that Jelani welcomed with open mind and heart.

The energy faded with the light, but no one moved for some time, drinking in the last bits of that feeling before they filtered away. Other than her momentary irritation with Djana for pulling politics at the last minute, she felt strong, healthy and so much better than she had when they had come. She could see by the faces that passed her that the same was true for the others. Even Crispy was smiling and chatting in a relaxed way, something that had been missing for several months.

Elliun was the only one that seemed out of sorts. He was still pouting after the punishment he had received for talking to an outsider, particularly that outsider. He knew better. If she did not make his punishment strong, he would be tempted to do something like that again. The clan could not be exposed, no matter what else happened. So he would just have to pout.

She knew ways to deal with that, too. Her stepmother did not raise a fool.

CHAPTER 21

CHIARA'S team wandered the woods until it became too dark to maneuver safely. The next morning they decided to go back out to see what they had missed.

"This tree wasn't here last night," Steve said, sounding a little skeptical.

"Good! I thought maybe it was just me. I've got it on vid." Janie clicked up her screen, showing a broad panorama shot of trees and more trees, not this river that now rushed and bubbled before them. "That hill, it wasn't there either. See? Just another fat fir."

Each of them revealed what they had captured the night before and none of it looked like the present terrain.

"What's this?" Artie asked, bending down to grab a handful of gray matter. "Ash? This smells burnt."

"Man, I didn't see any fire here. Unless they waited for a midnight orgy."

Chiara pursed her lips, knowing that what they wanted to capture on video had actually happened while they were standing right there. She could feel it in the very core of her body. *Somehow they blocked us. It must have been some kind of diversionary projection. Could it have been magic?*

That pained her the most.

The exact phenomenon that she wanted to capture, the magic of the elves, had been what kept them from filming. *Smarter than the average bear, now, aren't they?*

The small internal voice mocked her and she shut it down as quickly as she could. They returned to the lodge, their work done. If she was going to succeed on this one, it would have to be on the vortex site films alone.

But it's not the end of that. I can patch in some of those telephone interviews I did with rangers and so on. Flesh out the scope of the errant vortex bursts. It'll be all right.

It'll be all right.

She let herself become so confident that she spent the afternoon with Curran Tanner, taking a red bus trip through the narrow passages of the Going-to-the-Sun Road, pausing just a moment on the exact top of the Continental Divide, feeling like she really was on top of the world.

He made overtures about seeing her again, and on that score she was not so sure. Although Hunter's offer of reconciliation seemed dependent on her coming up with the elf story, she still had some hope that it might happen anyway.

But Curran cares for you just the way you are. And you've had fun every minute you've been with him. He's no social climber like Hunter. Why move backward?

Damn that nagging inner voice! She could not ignore it, though. Instead, she promised Curran they would stay in touch, and perhaps he would come to New York for a look at her mountains, made of concrete and steel instead of the beauty of nature.

When they returned to the lodge an angry phone message waited for her. Dan screaming like a banshee wanting to know what kind of virus she had put in the video she sent.

"What are you talking about? It played just fine."

"Well, it stopped playing just fine and we can't get it uploaded again. Even copies we had on separate servers won't play on the channel's website or the station broadcast cameras."

"What the hell?"

Chiara rubbed a hand over her forehead, tension building behind it like a volcano ready to blow. This damned shoot had been one problem from beginning to end. Who knew what had happened? Maybe it was more elf magic. Whatever. She was done worrying about it. She had the vortex show, and she would be happy with that.

The team met her at the door, heading to the lounge for a post job drinking session, but she decided she needed some alone time, just wanting to relax. After a long soak in a hot bath with luxurious dark floral bubbles, Chiara reluctantly dragged herself out of the tub and patted herself dry. It was the last night. Her suitcase sat, packed, on the top of the dresser, waiting for her to tuck those last minute pieces inside.

It had been a tough two weeks. The good news was that they had put together their rough cut and sent it off. At least production had found it acceptable, according to their email update, and they were busy polishing up the piece. Everything was finally all right.

Wrapped in the thick white towel, she wandered out to the bedroom. The window was open. Three floors up, no one was going to spy on her. The night air was cool, forcing her to hurry into her sleep shirt and even wrap into a bathrobe. The television remote lay on the end of the bed, and she grabbed it in passing, flipping the television on for some noise. She returned to the bathroom to dry her hair, only half listening to the announcer. It was not until she heard the word 'vortex' that she really focused on it, curiosity dragging her out into the room where she could hear it better.

What was going on?

The setting did not look familiar, and finally a scroll came across the bottom of the picture pointing out it was the Oregon Vortex, not hers. But the narrator's story seemed to come right along her line, talking about a surge of energy over weeks and months, and then cut to the Psychic Phenomena channel logo, the introduction to their Strange Happenings show.

Now all the cable channels had their own paranormal reality shows these days, and she was only one of many. But PP channel was one of her primary competitors.

How had they known? Surely this couldn't be intentional. Could it?

She could not take her eyes from the screen as the show's host explained the theory behind the vortex and led the camera through the trail into the House of Mystery, a structure very much like the one at the Montana Vortex. They even did the same experiments that the guide had shown Chiara, right down to the test to stand a broom up on its bristles on the steeply angled floor.

The upshot of the half hour program seemed to be that while some purely natural explanations were appropriate for some of the phenomena, optical illusions, or other normal hokum, that they could not prove or disprove or explain what happened in those spots where people appeared to be inches shorter or taller just by which end of the flat concrete they stood on. Exactly the results she and her team had found.

She did not even realize she was holding her breath until she suddenly gasped for air. This was her show. This was everything she had prepared. Without the proof of this mysterious elf clan, she had nothing more than PP had just shown the world. They had scooped her!

Her own network could not run the show she had put together without someone suggesting it was a lazy rip off of the PP program.

She let herself fall backward onto the bed, staring at the ceiling in confusion. What was she going to do now?

I ought to call Dan and let him know.

The 'right' thing, perhaps, but it certainly did not feel right.

The only saving grace of the moment was that Janie and the crew were too busy partying, celebrating the end of their long hours' of work, and they had not seen the evidence that it was all for nothing.

Her sixth sense had twigged indicating that they had been out there in the woods. The ritual the elf child had referenced taking place just beyond her sight. But she had nothing. No chance remained that she would be able to prove their existence. The Elf Clan of the Bitterroot Mountains would remain just another unsolved mystery.

A huge sigh racked her body. *So close.*

The thought of curling up into bed, under those thick comforters and never coming out appealed to her. But it would not solve anything. She needed to think. She could not do it here. After their week of fresh air and big sky, the lodge walls threatened to crush her and she did not feel like she could take in enough air to survive.

Instead of dressing for bed, she slipped into her outdoor gear, mindful that by this time of night it was nearly fifty degrees, and grabbed the keys to the sport utility vehicle from the dresser. Passing by the door to the lounge at an angle so she would not be noticed, she hurried outside and got into the vehicle, glad that they had parked it down the lot, out of sight of the door. A few short seconds later, she pulled away into the night, only half-sure where she was going.

Twenty minutes later, she was back at the site where she expected the ritual to take place. She parked the car off the road in a little stand of trees and shoved the key in her pocket so she would be sure to have a way back. Flashlight in hand, she half-walked, half-ran back through the woods in the direction they had gone to film this alleged ritual, determined to see for herself that this was an impossible dream.

Landmarks she had used before popped out at her as she made her way. The bent tree with the knot in it, the fallen tree trunk she had to straddle in order to get over it, the open clearing that suddenly appeared between her and the Whitefish River.

And then it hit her. That clearing had not been here the night of the ritual.

When they tried to approach this area they encountered a thick area of thorny plant growth that blocked their path, not this pristine clearing.

She shone the flashlight from one side to the other, stunned. Was this clan's magic so powerful that they really could prevent intrusion by outsiders like herself? *Extraordinary.*

How long had they been here? How had they protected themselves through the ages? How many more of them were there? She had so many questions and not nearly enough answers. No answers at all.

She walked up to the water's edge as the moonlight came full into the clearing from overhead, so she turned off the flashlight and looked first left and then right, studying the flow of the river, wondering why the ritual had occurred here at this particular place. Had all the animals of the forest gathered around, like in a child's movie? Did the Native Americans of the region participate as well? Janie's research and several phone calls had yielded nothing that indicated the two cultures were linked, though the Indian spokespersons had been particularly cagy when questioned. Who knew if they were protecting the elves, or themselves?

Ripples of awareness passed through her senses, alerting her to a change in the air, or at least in the dimension where she stood. Carefully, hardly daring to move, she lowered herself onto the wet bank and sat there, cross-legged, waiting to see what was trying to invite itself into her world.

Little by little, her eyes adjusted to the half-light. The breeze around her was cool but she had dressed warmly enough not to notice, much. She tipped her chin up, studying the trees around her, hundreds of years old, straight and strong. They had survived who knew how many winters, how many summers, the advent of Native Americans, the coming of the wagon trains, and the lumberjacks. Perhaps the actions of this elf queen and her followers had helped protect them. Chiara sincerely hoped so. This was one of the most beautiful stretches of land she had ever seen.

"We're glad you appreciate it."

A male voice drifted dreamily to her on the wind. She looked around sharply but saw no one.

"Show yourself!"

Nothing but one lone dove's plaintive coo's to break the silence.

Frustrated, Chiara started to get up.

"No, wait. Stay where you are."

Torn between obeying the unseen man and her natural tendency not to let others boss her around, Chiara hesitated, long enough to catch a glimpse of movement across the ten yard expanse of the river, a flicker of smoke and light that coalesced into the form of a well built man. The sight kept her in a seated position. "Who are you?"

Warm hazel eyes smiled at her. "I am Daven Talvi."

She tried to read him, all the while surreptitiously digging in her pocket for her cell phone so she could video this encounter. Her senses perceived a being of substance, not a ghost, who occupied real space there on the riverbank. His gaze went to her hand, and he gently waved an arm in her direction.

"Your device will not work. This is not a meeting for the purpose of exposing a people who need to be concealed, but an attempt to explain to you the way of the world."

Chiara ignored him and brought the phone out into the open, finding it drained of power. "So how did you do that, and why? Do you people think that getting your picture taken steals your soul?"

The man across from her broke into a rollicking laugh. "Chiara, some of us spent many years hiding in and among your people. We have no illusions about your mechanical devices."

"You know my name?"

"It was shared with us."

Realization came to her. "Lane Donatelli."

"Of course. He is one who guards the safety of this clan."

"A human? Who guards the elves? You're kidding me."

"Not at all. He has much invested here, and has proved valuable to us." A bit of a knowing apology entered his voice. "As you found the night we conducted our ritual."

"He constructed the barrier?"

"He is a technomage of many skills."

The outlines of the man shimmered in the moonlight, and for a moment, Chiara even wondered if she was really seeing what she thought she was seeing. "A t-technomage. Huh. Never heard that term."

"Perhaps no one has." He laughed again, a soft sound like warm caramel. "But Lane seems to like it."

Irritation seeping into her like the muddy wetness through her jeans, she wondered why he had appeared to her, if his only purpose was to toy with her and prove she was an idiot.

"I don't find you to be an idiot at all. Far from it. I think you are blinded by your ambition and your long hidden pain and loss."

Chiara blinked. She had not said that aloud. She knew she had not. How had he known what she thought? Just like the child, he was able to reach into her mind and decipher what she was thinking. She had been able to do this to unsuspecting others for years, but when she was the subject of the mind read, she found it significantly disturbing. Her muscles tensed, but she could not move.

"May I join you?" he asked, holding a hand out in her direction.

Not like I could stop you, apparently.

His answer came inside her mind, almost as if whispered over her shoulder, very close. *But I would respect your boundaries if you refused.*

"Whoa!" She scrambled to her feet, backing away quickly from the water, before he could get his hands on her. A moment later, she realized he had not moved. He sounded so real, so near, she had been sure he was right there.

What the heck? She had never seen an elf man up close. When would she get that chance again, huh? Someone might believe her eventually. Someone who mattered. Even if she had no scientific proof.

"I guess that would be okay."

She watched as the man seemed to float across the surface of the water on an arc of sparkling light. The transit was beautiful, reflecting the bands of stars overhead, visible here in the clearing, thanks to the lack of city lights. When he stepped ashore he snapped his fingers and the arc dissipated into bits of energy that spiraled away and dove into the ground.

I've never seen anything like that. Never.

A smile curled her lips into a welcoming posture. She could not help it. This elf, standing nearly six feet tall and with the shoulders of a football player, stood before her practically exuding goodwill. A sharp warning ribboned through her thoughts that he might be lulling her into submission before a strike, in the manner of a cobra, but she felt so comfortable and comforted that she could not even make herself react.

"I will not harm you, Chiara," he promised. "Far from it. I'd like to help you."

"What would have helped me would have been letting me get that story last week. Then I could get my career back on track and be able to feed myself."

He nodded thoughtfully. "You mean money."

Her brow scrunched into a knot. "Well, duh. That's how we do things in the real world. We need money."

He studied her a moment and then held out his hand. "May I take your hand?"

Suspicious, she hesitated, and then slowly extended her hand to his. "I'll get it back right?" she asked, trying to keep the mood light. What could he do? Drag her into a magic world? Become her Prince Charming? Bury her forever? *He said he wouldn't hurt me.* Right. Most men did, did they not?

He took her hand in his and then put his other hand atop it, closing his eyes. Energy flowed around him, growing larger, wider, until it encircled them both. She realized with a little thrill that they were inside a pulsating vortex, its energy sweeping around her, brushing her skin with an almost palpable touch. *Where's my damned camera when I need it? This is incredible.*

You do have a gift, came his voice in her head again. *You see so much, yet you see nothing at all.*

She let herself answer in thought speak as well. *That's all well and good, oh wise one, but it's really nonsense. I've heard the same doubletalk in a preacher's sermon and in a political speech. I see what I need to see.*

He squeezed her hand and her mind was suddenly filled with the image of herself as a teenager, in a crushingly small dark space, her arm and hips hurting, her head throbbing. A sound came from her left, a moan of pain so filled with agony that it hurt her, and she realized where she was and what was about to happen.

No! Please no...not this....

But he did not heed her protests or the growing nausea in her stomach. She turned her head in the direction of the sound and saw what she knew she would find. Her mother pinned to her seat with the distorted steering wheel of the car half buried in her chest. Her mother's fractured collarbone had torn through her skin, and she bled into the darkness. Sirens sounded in the distance, but Chiara knew they would be too late, too late. Her throat choked up with tears.

This is what drives you. Your guilt over not being able to save her. The fact that you lived. You aren't the one who killed her. The other driver was at fault. You were just a child.

Her mother's eyes stared into hers, at first tight with pain and tears of her own. Her mouth worked, but nothing came out. With great effort, her mother forced her own hand out to grab Chiara's, squeezing it tight, much in the same way Daven Talvi held it now.

"Mama," Chiara whispered, her heart torn in two again as she re-experienced the first loss in her life, the one that changed everything. She watched her mother's eyes as they changed from their pained look, to a sort of peace, and then gradually clouded over. She was gone, again.

I hate you for making me live through that again. You're horrible! Why would you do such a thing?

When she would have yanked her hand away, he held firm. *Wait. That isn't the worst of it.*

What? What could be worse than losing her mother again? She struggled to think what he might refer to. What happened next was the conversation she had with her mother's spirit after her mother's passing, that exchange of love and worry and wishes for a future for Chiara that her mother would never see. She could not go through that again, she could not. "No, please," she whispered.

But the tableau inexorably continued, her mother's voice sharing hopes, words of encouragement, reminding Chiara of good times they had and why she should focus on those times instead of this tragic moment. Tears choked Chiara's throat and she could not respond, even though she wanted to reassure her mother that everything was fine. *It's all right, Mama.*

The elf man would not let her go, though.

You took those precious words your mother gave you to hold in your heart and protect you until you should meet again, and you sold them.

That brought her up short. Chiara thought he intended to study human pain by experiencing it through her. But Daven fastened on the one thing she thought had saved her, the story that had launched her career.

My mother would have been proud of the skills I have developed. She would have acclaimed my rise to fame. She wanted me to do well. Defiant, she looked into his eyes, and found only compassion there.

"She would have wanted Bonny to grow up healthy, and happy," he said aloud.

A shiver ran through her. "Stop it."

"Don't you think she might not recognize Chiara DeLuna, the media celebrity? That's not the little girl she loved. By taking her last act of love for you and turning it into a means to feed your avarice, you denigrated everything that existed between you." He let go of her hand. "And you know this. It's eaten away at your heart for thirty years."

Mama? Could it be true?

She always felt as if she lost more that day than just her mother. But after that she was alone. She had to look out for herself. Who else would have? She had no choice.

You had to be brave. The words caressed and supported her. *It is as bad a thing to have no mother as it is to have one that is neglectful or abusive. But this does not define your life, unless you let it.*

The power of the vortex around them pulsed. Then it faded.

The elf man stared down into her eyes. She felt lost, as if she could not look away.

"You are still the woman you were born, even if you believe that life was torn away from you. You don't have to judge your worth by your stature in others' eyes. You have your own gifts, and could use them for many purposes."

Even as he spoke, she knew what he said was true. Her

meeting and friendship with Curran Tanner was evidence of that. He valued her for what she was. She had recognized that earlier in the day.

Although my celebrity certainly opened the door.

Perhaps so. But the woman he appreciates is the one you are inside.

Daven reached out and took her shoulders, holding them firmly, and she experienced a ripple of heat race through her from top to bottom. When it had passed, all she felt was contentment. He stepped back, seeming more distant than he really was, as if he were about to fade away into the mist.

"The clan will remain on these lands where they have lived for hundreds of years, as you humans mark them. We have our disputes and dramas, just as you do, often spilling over onto the cycle of nature. As you've seen, or at least suspected, the health of our clan is affected by the vortex, and when we are in balance, so it will be too."

"That seems…logical." She smiled. "Now is this where you ask me to forget all I've seen and heard and go back to my world, leaving yours alone?"

He caressed her cheek. "There is no need. Be well, Bonny Lang. Remember those who truly love you."

He raised his hand over her head, murmuring words she could not understand. Her brain began to fog up, and she felt woozy. When she next could gather her thoughts, she found herself in the sports utility vehicle on the road.

What am I doing here?

She could not remember why she sat there, parked on a dirt path, in the woods, keys in her hand. She must have wanted to investigate something, but she just could not recall what would bring her out in the middle of the night. Her phone lay beside her on the seat, but it gave her no clue. She started the car, still mystified, finding she did remember the way back to the resort. On the way there, she had the feeling her mother was a little angel sitting on her shoulder, looking out for her. It was a feeling she had not had for a very long time.

"Don't worry about me, Mama, I'm getting my life together, I promise," Chiara murmured. Then wondered why she did.

When she arrived back at the resort she found her crew in the lounge, still, and they marveled over her distressed and dressed state.

"I thought you were headed up for a hot bath and bed," Artie said.

Chiara considered that. "Yeah. Yeah, that's what I was going to do. That is what I did. Then I was watching the television while I got dressed, and...." Then she remembered what she had seen, the beginning of the end.

I'm not going to tell them today. They worked too hard. Tomorrow is plenty of time to get to that. Let's not ruin what's left of it.

"Well, I'm here now. Who's buying me a drink? And call me Bonny."

CHAPTER 22

"WHERE'S Elliun?"

"Where's Elliun?"

The question passed from voice to voice, mind to mind, spreading through the tree borne bowers of the elf clan, like foam skipping atop of river rapids. Max, pondering his fate alone in his own small bower room, looked down through the opaque walls to see Astan rush up from below, followed by Vez and a few others. The face of the queen's consort was contorted with worry.

"Max? Is Elliun with you?"

Max frowned and came to his door, wafting lightly down to the ground. "I left him with you after the ritual, just before the sun came up. Jelani had him by the hand. She said—"

Astan nodded. "I know what she said. That she needed to think over whether you were an appropriate guide for him." He put a congenial hand on Max's shoulder. "Myself, I have no doubt you are a fine teacher. But we will discuss that later. Elliun disappeared soon after our return to the tree house. No one can find him."

The support Astan gave him warmed Max through and through. He had not lost the respect of the clan leaders, at least not fully. *There is time enough to save my position. And my self worth.*

He did not exactly think that last thought in so many words, but that was the worry that had sickened him all through the ritual, had since he had allowed Elliun to slip from him and reveal clan secrets to the human woman. So much of his tenuous self esteem held to this one task he had accepted, even knowing it was an enormous responsibility. Perhaps just for that very reason. In order to overcome the prejudices against him, he had to do something bigger and better than everyone else.

Now he was in jeopardy again because of Elliun's stubborn misbehavior.

The area around them filled with elves running, calling Elliun's name. Lokni sent summonses out on the wind, while Rudra enchanted small water pixies to seek him out. "What can I do?" Max asked.

Vez looked over Astan's shoulder. "I don't know if Max is the one to ask, Astan. Maybe he's done enough to place us in harm's way. We're better off to look on our own."

Astan's jaw set like the granite of the Mission Mountains. "Don't tell me who I can trust, brother."

Vez physically backed off, his face getting a little pale at Astan's tone. "Just what the queen said—"

"Enough!" Astan snapped and took a sharp intake of breath. "Max, if he comes to you, please take him to Jelani at once." He turned on his heel and marched away, Vez and the others on his heels for a moment. Once they were out of Max's hearing, they exchanged some heated words, and then Vez and his companions went left into the forest while Astan headed back in the direction of the tree house.

So that's how it was.

With his heart breaking, Max skinned back up the tree only long enough to collect his bow and arrows and a pack of food. He shrugged on a warm jacket and shoved the food in his pockets, slinging the bow over his shoulder. They did not think he could find Elliun? Who else could possibly know better how the boy's mind worked?

He started in the direction of the path out to the road, guessing that Elliun would try to trick those who expected him to run deeper into the dark woods. He had nearly reached the path when he saw Lane's red truck parked where he had left it before the ritual. Lane was not in it, but Crispy sat slumped, sleeping, in the front seat. Max ran lightly over to the driver's side and knocked on the window.

Crispy shot up in the seat, mouth gaping, but when he saw it was Max, he put a hand over his heart and rolled down the window. "You scared me to death. I thought it was Bigfoot or something."

"He has been gone from these woods since the *Donoma* has been in flux. Where is the Lane?"

Crispy gestured off in the direction from which Max had come. "He decided to stay with Jelani, once she locked her gun up. She was pretty upset." Crispy blinked a double take at Max, as if he had not seen him before. "Elliun isn't with you, is he?"

"No. I haven't seen him since the ritual. But the queen truly hurt him with her words of discipline, I could feel it in him. He did not believe she loved him anymore."

Crispy's teeth sunk into his lip and his eyes filled with tears. "Poor kid. I know what that feels like."

"Why are you not searching for him?"

The human cleared his throat. "They told me they didn't need me. That I might just hold them back." He shrugged. "I don't know. Maybe they were right. I haven't been doing well lately." He looked around the interior of the vehicle. "I actually felt better once I got back in this little space."

As Crispy spoke, Max heard much in his tone that echoed his own feelings. The fact that such a kind soul as Crispy's had been found wanting and insufficient, like his own, just increased his resentment. "No," he said. "It's not true. We are not useless!"

"What do you mean, *we*? You're...." Crispy hesitated a moment as if processing the words. "You, too?"

Max nodded, fighting his own tears.

With a sigh, Crispy reached to pull the driver's door handle. "Want to come in here with me and wait?"

Max stared at the open door, the inviting seat, and then took a step back. "No. I'm going to find him. Do you want to come with me?"

Hardly realizing he held his breath, waiting, Max wished and wished that Crispy would come with him. He was willing to go on his own, but he was feeling a little shaky. Even Crispy would be good company. They could keep up each other's spirits.

Finally Crispy gave a half smile. "Sure, why not? What's the worst thing that could happen? That we get attacked by grizzly bears or abducted by aliens?"

As his companion shoved his thin arms into a thick hoodie, Max considered the two options and decided the bear would be more likely, but he knew that bear tended to move away from areas frequented by humans in the summer months. He did not really know the hunting patterns of aliens. Perhaps next time he saw The Lane, he could ask for clarification.

Crispy joined him, and together they turned east, heading for the top of the nearest mountain. With Crispy by his side, Max might be able to enlist one other powerful ally in the hunt for the missing prince, Hawky, anything to give them an edge.

* * *

EVEN with the red-tailed hawk taking to the sky and providing small amounts of guidance, in the eccentric manner of hawks, Max was not Elron and he had no instant way of communication with the bird. The trail was still hit and miss. Several hours later, the two of them exhausted, he and Crispy sat on a large boulder, sharing the remains of a granola bar Crispy found in his pocket.

"He's a tricksy one," Crisp muttered.

"Yes." Max closed his eyes, trying to sense the boy once again. After all the hours they had spent together, he had to believe that he had a psychic connection with him. *But I certainly don't feel it.* Perhaps the child had the power, like Daven Talvi, to block others' minds, thinking he was only protecting himself, though he was really putting himself in harm's way.

Why couldn't Astan see him, with his sixth sense of constructing situations? Why hadn't Daven or the other mages found him? These things Max did not know, but his loose connection with others in the clan told him that the child remained missing.

"You know, I think they're right, Max. I'm no good at this stuff. I can hardly find my own way in life, much less anyone else's." Crispy looked around at the open sky above and landscape below, and then crossed his arms with a little shiver.

Max pursed his lips a moment, thinking. "But The Lane says you saved him and Astan and Iris, back during the troubles. That you were the only one able to break free of the sorcerer in time to save them."

Crispy looked away. "I...I don't want to talk about that."

Puzzled, Max shifted his seat on the rock. "If you hadn't done what you did, the queen would not have survived. We would have all been lost to Bartolomey's evil."

Crispy did not reply, just stared off into the distance, his face set hard as if trying to prevent those memories from getting back in.

If Crispy was a hero, why did he fight it so much? Wasn't being heroic a good thing? All of the heroes in Lane's online stories were good looking, gifted and wonderful. The same was true of heroes in the elf traditions. Heroes were good.

Max was confused, as he often was when first confronted with human behavior. Maybe he had misunderstood the story, when Lane told it, but he remembered that Rotiner, who had the power to control minds of others, freezing and hypnotizing them into inaction and had everyone paralyzed with fear. Crispy was the one who came forward to destroy him so the others could live, and this allowed Astan to arrive in time to save the queen. What could be wrong with that?

The pain blocking Crispy's acceptance of his well meant words felt genuine, and he recognized a similar pain in his own heart. How did one prove himself strong enough, smart enough? Max did not need to be a celebrated hero living through the ages in songs around the central hearth. All he wanted was to be recognized for the good *nian* he was, and for the effort he put out.

His thoughts now were with Elliun and his well being, and how that would affect Max's standing in the clan. If something happened to Elliun, would the clan continue to blame his teachings or something he had failed to teach? Would he be cast out? He knew what the Elders said happened to an elf who lived apart from others of his kind. Even though Grigor had seemed to thrive on his own, everyone knew now that he had been receiving clandestine assistance through Veraena and Bartolomey. If Max was exiled, he would certainly have no such choices. He would live alone, and then he would die.

The thought saddened him, but even as it became part of his consciousness, he rejected it. This was not his fault. He knew he had done the best work he could with a very young *nian*, who was just feeling the need to stretch his wings. They both deserved the chance to continue.

Elliun, where are you?

He closed his eyes and sat very still, picturing the boy's face in his mind's eye. *If only the energy from the earth would recognize individual signatures, the way the wizards could in Lane's game.*

The longer he sat, a small point of distress coalesced in his midsection and slowly grew in size and sound until it filled his abdomen, and finally the scream came out his mouth. "Help!"

Crispy jumped off the rock, staring at him in shock. "What?"

Max found himself trembling, breathing hard and scared to death. "N-Not me," he gasped. "Elliun."

"Where?" The human looked over the edge of the rock at the valley below, and then all around as if the child would appear momentarily.

Max tried to channel the feelings inside him into a particular direction, hoping to answer that question for himself. Elliun was certainly of Daven's line. That mental voice was the best clue yet. Surely that cry will have been heard by many other sensitives in the clan. Perhaps they can get to him sooner.

The panic seemed to emanate from the northeast, completely in the opposite direction Max had expected, up toward the region the humans called Glacier.

"Come on!" he cried, starting down the hill at a run. Crispy stumbled after him, holding his backpack by one flapping strap. Max did not let thoughts interfere with his senses but homed in on that feeling of desperation, letting it flood through him and pull him along. He ran and kept running, oblivious to his companion's breaths which became more ragged as the land passed, down the mountain and around some heavy rocks piled at its foot.

An earlier avalanche must have spilled rocks in all directions here, and Max needed the adrenaline pumping through his veins to spur him on across a second pile of rough, broken rocks, some nearly half as tall as he was himself. There he found Elliun with his back against the wall of the mountain very near the entrance to a cave, a semi-circle of six large gray wolves around him, growling and nipping in his direction, inching closer.

"Max!" Elliun cried in relief.

Crispy staggered around the corner and stopped when he saw the predicament the child was in. Gasping for air, he leaned on the rocks, an expression of confusion on his face. When Max gestured at him, he moved back around the rock to a place more protected.

"Hold still, Elliun," Max warned. He could not understand the situation, though it lay right in front of him. Wolves did not attack humans as a rule, and they attacked elves even less often. Max could not remember a tale of such an attack in his own lifetime, but he had heard the Elders of the Circle talk about one. What had Elliun done to provoke them? More importantly, what would it take to defuse them?

The wolves were so focused on their prey that they did not even spare a glance for Max, who had paused at the edge of the rock. He inched closer, trying to find a point of entry that would not involve himself being shredded before he could reach Elliun, who now had tears in his eyes.

"I'm so sorry," the young prince whispered.

"Don't worry about that now, Elliun. Just stay calm." Max studied the wolves' posture, and found it odd that they would not respond to a threat from behind them. "Something's not right."

Crispy's head popped up from behind the rock where he was hiding. "Distemper," he said.

"What?"

"Distemper. It's a canine disease. In the wild, wolves could pick it up from drinking contaminated water. It makes them act strangely. We had a pair up at the injured animal shelter. They lose proper fear responses, and become aggressive in situations where usually they won't engage."

"How did you repair them?

Crispy sighed. "We didn't. They had to be put down."

"Where did you put them?"

"No, Max, they had to be killed. There was no other way."

Crispy's words tasted of regret, and Max frowned as he studied the wolves. Normally a mutual respect shared between elves and wild predators meant they left each other alone. It was considered bad taste, bad karma among the elves to kill one, though other animals used for food were considered fair game.

"How did this start, Elliun? Tell me without moving."

"I—I was looking for a place to hide, and I thought this cave would be okay, but one of the wolves was in there. He backed me out, and when I looked outside, the others were all here, too."

The wolf closest to Elliun moved in, jaws snapping as he growled. Only inches away, Max could read the effort to hold still, to appear unthreatening, in the boy's every muscle. Max hesitated, startled when the real noise began behind him.

"Hey! Over here!" Crispy yelled as he stepped out from behind the rock. "Here, Fido. Here, doggy, doggy!"

The wolves turned for the first time, noticing that they had human company, and bared their teeth in Crispy's direction as an indication of how welcome a human might be. The three closest to Max seemed to ignore him, but turned to challenge Crispy with loud, spine jangling howls.

Now Max was truly torn. He owed The Lane a great debt of love and friendship, and he could not let his dear friend come to harm. But neither could he allow Elliun to be hurt in any way. Vez's face popped into his mind, saying that Max had done enough, implying that he was worthless when it came to his responsibilities as the guardian of the young prince. He looked back and forth between the two, knowing he might have to sacrifice one for the good of the other.

Crispy spared him a glance for just a moment. "This is your

time to shine, brother! "Do what you have to do. Save him!"

Max heard the words, their finality sinking into his heart. *I know which one, though it hurts my heart to choose.*

He drew the short dagger from his boot that he had been given by Astan when he was appointed to this position, making sure his hand clenched tight around it. With a loud yell, he launched himself into the air, knowing he would sail over at least two of the beasts. He did so, though they reared up, trying to bite at his feet overhead. He landed nearly astride the one closest to Elliun, and had to do a fast two step to angle himself into the inches between them.

That set the wolf off, and he jumped on Max, claws digging deep into his shoulders as its teeth snapped and tore at his jacket collar, trying for his jugular. The extra weight of the wolf on Max's slight frame shoved him backward into Elliun and the rocks. The boy yelped beneath him, but there was nothing Max could do. His face was next to the wolf. The fetid breath of the beast filled his nose and lungs. One arm was bent at the elbow trying to keep the wolf's teeth from tearing his face to bits as its paws raked his chest and the other struggled with the dagger trying to get it in position.

Yes. There.

The dagger slipped between the ribs of the wolf, finding its heart. It pulled away from Max with a piteous cry, and then collapsed. The wolf nearest them turned its attention first to Max, as if it would take up where its companion had failed, but instead leaned down to sniff its dead companion with a small whine.

"Elliun, are you all right?" Max forced out, his breaths agony after his thin ribs had been bruised under the wolf's weight.

"Mm-hmm."

He did not sound like he was all right, and Max felt him trembling through every place their bodies touched. "It will be fine, Elliun. I'm here to protect you."

"Good," was all he said, but some tone in that single word signified a change in the respect the young one held for him. Max got to his feet, keeping Elliun behind him, taking a minute to survey the scene.

One wolf was down, its companion cowed. The other four watched Crispy, some ten feet from Max, standing tall on his right leg, his left leg raised, bent at the knee, and his arms spread over his head, his hands bent like birds' beaks, making some strange keening noise that seemed to climb right up Max's rattled spine.

"Is he casting a spell?" Elliun whispered.

"I honestly have no idea, little man."

Whatever it was he did, the wolves only tolerated a few minutes of it before they slunk away, baying, into the woods, leaving the dead one behind. Once they were quite gone, Crispy relaxed into his normal stance, leaning against the rock for support.

"What was that?" Max asked.

"The Crane. Kung Fu Fighting." A proud smile affixed itself on Crispy's pale face and did not seem to shake loose. "But you're bleeding."

Max noticed for the first time that the front of his jacket was soaked with blood, and he felt a bit woozy. "I'll be fine," he said. "Come, we should let the others know Elliun is safe."

"I should carry that cell phone Lane got me," Crispy said with regret. "But I don't want to get cancer."

"Cell phones give you cancer?"

"Everything gives you cancer." Crispy rolled his eyes.

Max stumbled as they moved forward. Crispy grabbed onto him. "Let me help you, Max. You saved us all."

"I just did what I had to do." The pain in his ribs was exquisite, and every breath hurt to inhale.

Crispy's smile was strange and faraway. "Sometimes that's harder than it appears. But the choice is the easiest in the world. You did the right thing."

Lightheaded, Max could only nod as Crispy half-carried him up the hill.

"Saving those you love is the most important act you can do," Crispy said. Then he repeated it over and over, like a mantra.

Max realized Crispy had turned some sort of corner in his healing process, or perhaps Max was just hallucinating. He really did not feel like himself at all.

They followed Elliun to the top of the hill, where Elliun let go long enough to give a fine approximation of an eagle's cry, which was echoed a few moments later from down in the valley.

He turned to Max, his eyes widening a bit as he saw the front of the jacket, his lip quivering a moment, but he took his arm again, standing up straight. "They'll be here in just a moment. Stay with us, Max."

His words seemed to come from far away. Max struggled to hear them, but they seemed to blend into the fog creeping in around him. An eagle cried out on the breeze, or was it a hawk? He could vaguely see one flying above them, a dark silhouette against the blue sky. But as he watched, it became a flag, flickering from blue to gray, sitting on top of a hill, and he was trying to capture it and keep it from the enemy.

Then someone was holding him, singing to him, but he could not quite hear the voice. Warmth came through with that song, telling him he had done well. Other voices grew loud around him, and he felt himself being lifted up, but he heard nothing more.

* * *

"ELLIUN?"

The word came from his lips first, before he even had his eyes open, while he was still dreaming, thinking he had been torn open by wolf claws. The sense of danger surrounded him, and he knew he had to protect the prince.

"Hush, Max. Elliun is right here."

Max forced his eyes open to find Astan Hawk sitting by his bedside. Though a look around the room told him he was not in his own bower at all, but in the queen's tree house. *In the queen's own bed.* He struggled to get up, feeling unworthy, but Astan laid a hand on him and kept him still.

"No, you don't. If anything happens to you now, Jelani will kill me. And I don't intend to have that happen, not at all."

He smiled, and it was a warm and wonderful smile. Warmth came from the hand that lay on Max's arm, like a web of light that crept along each tendon, each muscle, each limb, making each whole again.

"But—"Max found his voice raspy and his breaths short and painful. He looked down to see his chest was swathed in thick bandages. "Crispy?"

"Fine, too." That smile went on. "You saved them both, or you both saved Elliun, I'm not sure which. He can't stop talking about the bravery of each of you."

"All…safe. Good." His eyelids were heavy again, and he thought he slept. Dark dreams of snapping teeth and the smell of blood came to him now and again, but when he woke a second time, the queen herself was there with him, changing his bandages and adding fresh herbs next to his skin for healing. They smelled sweet, though their juices burned a little.

"There you are," she said, a small smile lighting up her face. "We thought you might leave us, which would be such a shame after all you've done." She finished her work quickly and then covered him with a light blanket.

"Milady, forgive me for being in your bed. I would be fine in my own—"

She held up a hand. "Not another word. I won't hear of it." She reached to the table beside the bed and brought forth a bowl of soup that smelled more delicious than any Max had smelled before. "Eat." She fed him half a spoonful. "It's red lentil with Indian spices. Lane brought this from Good Foods down in Missoula. It's got everything an elf warrior needs to replenish his strength."

Max eyed her, too weak to do more than eat the soup she fed him. He found it amazing, with flavors he had never had before. Before he finished, Elliun bounded into the room behind his mother, breaking into a grin when he saw Max was awake.

"Finally," he said. "I've been waiting for my lessons."

When Max would have apologized, Jelani cut him off and spoke to Elliun. "Hush now. No teasing. You know Max is resting still. Your grandfather will be here again this evening to help his healing along." A bit of mischief entered her eye. "Perhaps Djana has some task for you to do...."

A look of horror shot across the young *nian*'s face. "Mother, no! Don't send me there. Not again."

Jelani winked at Max. "That's true. Ever since you came home safely, Djana and the others just haven't been quite happy."

He wondered what she meant by that. They did not want him to return? Would she ban him from the clan? He glanced around the room, wondering what it all meant. She nursed him back to health herself, in her own bed. How, then, would the clan be unhappy with him?

She must have seen the troubled look he knew he wore, because she sent the boy out of the room to play instead.

"Have I done w-wrong?" he asked her.

"Wrong? No, not at all. Quite the opposite, dear Max. You've justified every bit of trust we ever put in you. You saved our son, nearly at the cost of your own life. We owe you everything." Her eyes filled with tears, as she squeezed his hand. "Everything."

Still confused, he glanced after Elliun. She seemed to read his mind.

"Oh, Djana and the others? They're without a scapegoat at the moment and they just don't know how to live like that." She chuckled to herself. "Oh, and believe me, I should know."

She finished feeding him the soup and left him to rest. Max started feeling better about things and felt even better when Daven visited later in the day.

"I believe you'll be up and around in a few more days at this rate, Max," Daven said. "You have had the best of care, a collaborative effort of all those who love you."

"Thank you," Max said softly. His breathing came easier now, though his ribs, broken in the wolf attack, would take time to heal properly.

"How do you feel now about your role?" Daven asked.

"What do you mean?"

"You worried that you could not care for Elliun, or teach him all he needed to know. Do you still believe this?"

Max cocked his head. "He was nearly lost because I couldn't control him."

"*Nearly* being the key word." Daven leaned back in his chair, an amused look on his face. "Personally I tend to think that the young are better left to learn on their own, with a bit of guidance. Sometimes then they learn their most important lessons."

Max's eyebrow shop up in a quizzical expression.

"I believe he's discovered that running away and being alone in the woods has serious risks and consequences," Daven replied. "Now that he's seen what happens with his own eyes."

"Oh, that. I suppose so." Max nodded a little, shifting in the bed to a more comfortable position.

"But you've taught him a much more important lesson, Max, one that could not be taught in a book or a lecture. This lesson could be taught only from the heart. Do you know what it is?"

The way Daven looked at him, Max knew this was something very important, and he hesitated to speak afraid he would get it wrong. "What is it, Daven?"

"My dear Max, you've taught him the meaning of courage, and honor, and responsibility, through the power of your personal sacrifice. Putting aside one's own life to serve another, this is the greatest gift we can give."

Max studied the pain in Daven's eyes, and knew that Daven, too, had chosen to serve others even at the risk, and loss, of his personal life, dreams, and hopes. For Daven to share this with Max was high praise indeed. His cheeks flushed, and he struggled for words.

"I—I am happy to do it. To serve the clan."

Daven laid his hands on Max, sharing his own strength, as a mage could do, building up Max's energy. "You have made us all proud, son. Now take care of yourself, so you can get back to your job. The prince needs his guardian. And we don't want it to be anyone else but you."

"Yes, Daven, I will," Max said, finally able to smile.

Daven rubbed his shoulder, as he stepped from the room.

Left alone, Max pondered all of the things that had been said. Instead of finding him a freak of nature, as the Elders always made him feel, he was being accepted. It might be, as Lane often said, that it was because their little family was filled with freaks of nature and Max just fit in.

For whatever reason, he now belonged. He did not have to hide what he was any longer. His value was in himself and he could be proud of what he had done.

But most of all, Max realized that he had become part of a family at last, one that appreciated him and his gifts.

He would never be alone again.

THE END

About the Author

LYNDI ALEXANDER dreamed for many years of being a spaceship captain, but settled instead for inspired excursions into fictional places with fascinating companions from her imagination that she likes to share with others. She has been a published writer for over thirty years, including seven years as a reporter and editor at a newspaper in Homestead, Florida. Her list of publications is eclectic, from science fiction to romance to horror, from tech reporting to television reviews. Lyndi is married to an absent-minded computer geek. Together, they have a dozen computers, seven children, and a very full house in northwestern Pennsylvania.

* * *

Clan Elves of the Bitterroot Series:

THE ELF QUEEN
[Book I]

THE ELF CHILD
[Book II]

THE ELF MAGE
[Book III]

THE ELF GUARDIAN
[Book IV]

www.ingramcontent.com/pod-product-compliance
Lightning Source LLC
Chambersburg PA
CBHW021010180626
46814CB00003B/1234